"A joyride
—Rob Neufeld, *Asheville Citizen-Times*

"The best novel by a local author that I've read in years"
—Cecil Bothwell, author, *The Prince of War, Whale Falls*

"An utterly delightful story!"
- Jill Jones, *Bloodline,* and 10 other novels

"I stayed up reading 'til 3 AM to see how it turned out!"
– Jennifer Fitzgerald, editor, Black Mountain News

"Loved it, loved it, loved it! What a hilarious and informative book. Beautifully written. The ending, with all the time travelers racing towards the same tooth, was my favorite part. A very funny if naive protagonist, and really interesting to see young Nina Simone, Elvis, and others in Black Mountain history make their way through the story.
—Freesia McKee, poet and organizer

"I loved the time travel stuff, and the names! Goodness, the names! And the hilarity of the tooth-as-portal-key device. I cracked up over the conglomeration of folks trying to get into the dentist's office.
I sooooo want this to be a play!
—Rev. DiAnna Ritolla

THE ELVIS TOOTH

Copyright © 2013 by Jerald Pope
Published by Pope's Nose, an imprint of
Hare Brand Ideas, Swannanoa, NC, USA
All rights reserved
Printed in America
ISBN: 978-0-9858787-7-1

See more at: harebrandideas.com

Other books by Jerald Pope:

Madeleine Claire and the Dinosaur
Step Back in Time
The Minute Elf
An Early Appalachian Coloring Book

THE ELVIS TOOTH

*by
Jerald Pope*

Table of Contents

PART ONE: *June 19, 1948*

Pellom's Time Shop
The Corner Cafe
The Dance Hall
Jail
The Depot
The Bus Station
Avena's Bowling Alley
The Pix
Back to Dixie
A Black Mountain College Commentary
The Un-Jailbreak
A Walk Across Town
Roseland Gardens
A Walk Along the Creek
Desperados
The Montreat Gate

PART TWO: *July 23, 1975*

The Montreat Gate, Later
The Monte Vista
Pellom's Time Shop
Doctor Love
Pellom's Time Shop

PART THREE: *August 21, 2013*

Pellom's Time Shop
Town Hardware

Illustrations

Fire Station and City Hall, circa 1961, page 30
The Depot, circa 1948, page 38
Avena's bowling alley, page 52 *painting by Jerald Pope*
The PIX, page 62
Funeral parlor, page 84 *painting by Jerald Pope*
Dancing at Roseland Gardens, page 94
Montreat Gate, page 130
Monte Vista Hotel, 1940's, page 136
John Pellom in the Time Shop, 2013, page 186
Town Hardware, page 190 *painting by Jerald Pope*

"Midway on our life's journey,
I found myself in dark woods,
the right road lost."

~Dante, *The Inferno*

PART ONE: June 19, 1948

2 Jerald Pope

The Elvis Tooth 3

PELLOM'S TIME SHOP

"Can I help you?"

The man (who was decidedly – what? Sixty years younger than he had been – when? A minute ago?) took off his glasses and wiped them on a clean cotton rag he pulled from behind the counter.

"I…. I'm not sure. Say, when I walked in here, there was an old guy. It was you, wasn't it? Weren't you…. well, pretty old and kind of …. bald?"

The young man smiled wryly and placed the thick wire-rimmed spectacles back on his face. His wavy black hair glistened with oil. "Could be. When did you walk in?"

"What do you mean? Just now."

"No, *when* did you come in? What year?"

"What year? Now. This year. 2013." I was suddenly sweating, which I was sure I hadn't been a minute ago.

The less-than-old man whistled through his teeth. "And how'd I look?"

"Well, I'd say you looked older. Substantially older. Hey, what is this, a magic shop?"

I looked around the tiny store. "Pellom's Time Shop" it said in backwards letters on the front window. The counter, the shelves, the floor, every horizontal space was neatly arranged with clocks: alarm clocks, pocket watches, wristwatches, pendant watches, wall clocks, cuckoo clocks. Three grandfather clocks stood in huddled conversation toward the back, where a small sunlit window and a single hanging light bulb illuminated an immaculately ordered workbench.

I remembered seeing it from across the street. Cherry Street in Black Mountain, North Carolina. I was here to get married. It was just my fiancée, Clarice, and her parents right now. The rest of our party would start arriving tomorrow. We had come early to scout out the place and have a little alone time before the madness started. Don't ask me why her folks had joined us. And it's not like they were staying in the same room with us. They were staying in the room right next door. Van and Ursula had had their honeymoon in this same little mountain town thirty years earlier. They'd been coming back every year since. They wanted to share.

Wandering the town, I had spotted the little clock shop. My passion is old things, especially old pocket watches. This started when my great-grandfather died and my grandma gave me his father's watch: a silver and gold monstrosity the size of a goose egg with a fob braided from my great-grandmother's red hair. It was a rare and precious gift. And at ten years old, I couldn't wait to take it apart. What amazed me and captured my heart forever was the intricate engraving the maker had done on the *inside* of the watch. Such beauty where no one would see it! That watch was my key to the past. I became a history major, wrote my thesis on "the mechanics of railroad time-tables during the Civil War," and fell into a job doing irrelevant historical research for movies and the History Channel. "Irrelevant" because most people wouldn't know a peplum from a mutton sleeve. Or care, if they did.

"Why'd you ask what year I came in? What year do *you* think it is?"

"I think it's what the calendar says it is," he said, pointing over his shoulder. There, a remarkably fresh looking funeral home calendar, with a picture of Jesus smiling and opening a gate, said it was June, 1948.

"No offense, but you're a little bit of an eccentric, aren't you?"

I picked up the rag he had wiped his glasses with and wiped the sweat from my face. He snatched the rag from my hand, but smiled.

"Maybe, maybe not. Time will tell."

"Well, it's been – interesting. You got a nice – an interesting shop. Magic – not really into it. So, I gotta go. People waiting."

"Um hm. I'll be here."

"Okay. Bye." I pushed open the door, which was cleaner, newer than it had been when I walked in, and stepped out on the street.

Cherry Street was just as crowded as it had been when I entered Pellom's, but the crowd was different. Men were now wearing hats, mostly straw, but all the old-fashioned Panama-type; not a ball cap to be seen. And quite a few of them now wore jackets, even in the heat of a North Carolina summer's day. Some even sported ties, fat short ties that barely came down to the waistband of their pants, which were decidedly high-rise. Some men had on sport shirts in odd colors of gray, green, and maroon. One fat man had on a Hawaiian shirt with a killer pattern of blue and yellow hula girls. But T-shirts, cargo shorts, hiking boots, and sandals, the usual American summer attire, were nowhere to be seen.

The women were dressed just as strangely. In the first place, they all wore dresses. Flouncy skirts that came to mid-calf. Quite a few obviously had on petticoats. And every one of them had on gloves! White gloves! And funny straw hats in different colors.

There were just as many children, the girls in dresses like their mothers, but without the hats and gloves. Many of the boys were wearing shorts: funny, large high-waisted affairs – some with suspenders. Several of them had hats or caps, and I swear one kid had on a beanie, with an honest-to-god propeller on it. Not a phone or a video game to be seen, although the beanie kid did have a slingshot sticking out of his back pocket. They were laughing, chattering, gawking. They seemed genuinely happy and excited to be where they were: the opposite of the bored, elsewhere children I was used to.

People were talking, nodding, tipping their hats. Lots of men were just sitting on benches or leaning against walls. Children stood patiently while their parents chatted. These were not my people.

The street, which had been blacktopped when I entered Pellom's, was now paved in bricks. The cars moving slowly through the crowds were huge shiny beetle-like contraptions, looking exactly like they belonged, well, in 1948.

I noticed the crowd was, for the most part, moving in one direction – up hill. Then a loud, piercing scream stabbed the air. I jumped like someone had thrown ice water down my back, but the crowd seemed unperturbed. The scream came again, followed by a loud whoosh, and I placed the sounds: a train, not a diesel, but a steam driven train. A burly-looking steam engine was leaving the bustling station at the bottom of the hill. A station that had been a half-hearted little craft store thirty minutes ago. Now I could see the train, blowing smoke and steam, pulling away from the station with ten or twelve passenger cars. Passenger cars?

A lump of panic rose in my throat, threatening to choke me. Where, exactly, was my wife-to-be? Where were my potential new in-laws? Where was my new car? It was a 2013 Land Rover Defender Hybrid and I really loved it. I really loved Clarice, too, of course. The jury was still out on the in-laws.

I grabbed the arm of a man waiting to cross the street. "Excuse me," I said. "Sorry. But, can you tell me what today is?"

"The date?" He mildly pulled his arm from my grip. He had a trim little moustache and a cigarette dangling from his mouth. "Well, it's June something. The nineteenth, I think."

"Uh huh, good. And the year?"

He took the cigarette out of his mouth and gave me a look. "Are you kidding me, Mister?"

"No. Yes. I mean, please. The year is…?"

"Jeez. 1948. That's A.D., in case you were wondering."

"Okay. Okay, 1948. Thanks. Appreciate it."

He shook his head and continued across the street.

"Must be kind of a shock," a voice said behind me. I turned too quickly and almost knocked down the slick-haired man from the clock store. "Careful, pal," he said. "You look like you need to sit down."

"What is going on?" I grabbed him by his shirt-front and pulled his face close to mine. "Where did everybody go?"

"Everybody's right here. But I expect they're not the everybodies you mean. Let go of my shirt and don't spit in my face. You don't want to draw attention to yourself."

"Why? Why not?! I'm obviously going crazy! I'm a crazy man! That's what we crazy people do, we draw attention." I let him go and turned to the street. It was still there. Still the same. Still wrong. I shouted, "Hey, look! Crazy man here!"

He grabbed my shoulder in a surprisingly painful grip and turned me away from the curious faces looking our way. "You really don't want to do that. There's a logical explanation for what's going on, if you'll just calm down."

"Good, a logical explanation. I like the sound of that. How, logically, does a guy who's minding his own business, on a little vacation, a little wedding, turn around and suddenly… suddenly what? See, that's where the logic fails me. Suddenly, a hundred years back in time?"

"Oh, it's not a hundred years. More like sixty, sixty-five."

"Well, that makes me feel better, Mister… Pellom? Are you Pellom?"

"That's me. What's your name, pal?"

"Odell. Odell Lutz. Holy Jeez, I won't even be born for another quarter century!"

"Okay, Odell, calm down a bit. Hows about we get a drink?" He dragged me back to the sidewalk, pulled the door to his shop closed, and, keeping my elbow firmly in grasp, started up the street.

"Pellom, shouldn't you lock…?"

"What for?" he said. We walked up the street and he pushed open the door to a little café on the corner that hadn't been there ten minutes ago. That probably hadn't been there since the middle of the last century. I held firmly on to the hope that this Pellom, who was in actual fact a dealer in time, could deal me out of this crazy game I had stumbled into.

10 Jerald Pope

THE CORNER CAFÉ

A screen door with a metal soda ad in the middle was the only door, there being no air conditioning to keep inside. The place smelled of onions and hamburger and it was busy, but we found two empty stools at the counter.

"Hey, Dorcas. Sudsy," he said to the couple that stood behind the counter, both dressed in white uniforms. Sudsy had a white barracks cap on his head and a lit cigarette in his mouth. "Bring me a Dr Pepper. And my friend here will have…?"

"A beer," I said. "A large one of those Pisgah Pale Ales, if you have it."

Sudsy put down the glass he was wiping. "You mean a *root* beer, doncha, Mister?" He blew smoke out of the side of his mouth.

"'Course he does," the old man said, patting me on the shoulder.

"'Nother one of your Yankee friends, John?" Dorcas, who had patently artificial yellow hair, grinned at me.

"No, no. He just got to town from…?" They all paused and looked at me.

"Knoxville." I replied, weakly.

"That was the Statesville train, just come in. From the East." Sudsy said. "You on your way home? Get lost? Miss your train?"

"Just get us the drinks, Sudsy. Mind your own beeswax," John said. "He thinks he's gotta keep track of every stranger that hits town."

"Hard to do in the summertime," Dorcas said, taking out her own cigarette. "So many people nowadays. Since the War, y'know."

"We had Germans here. During the War. I ain't kiddin' neither." Sudsy flicked his ash on the floor behind the counter and pumped some brown syrup into a sculpted parfait glass. "I seen 'em, right in town."

"Prisoners of war, and you know that." John said. "Everybody knows that."

"Okay, John," I growled. "What in hell is going on here?"

"No need for that sorta filthy talk," Dorcas said, grinning no longer. She took a big drag off her cigarette and held the smoke in, just as she was holding her newly formed bad opinion of me.

"Yeah, Mister Knoxville Yankee," Sudsy chimed in, also still not smiling. "Take your dirty mouth somewhere else if you're gonna talk that way. This here's a family joint."

"Tell you what," I said, pulling a five from my wallet and slapping it on the counter. "I'll take my mouth and my business elsewhere, okay?"

John put his hand on the bill and slid it off the counter. "Your money's no good here."

"No, I'm paying."

"I mean it. Your particular money is not good here," he said and pointed to a dollar bill taped to the mirror behind the counter. It was a large silver certificate like I hadn't seen in… well, ever.

"Oh," I said.

"I got it," John said, tossing a quarter on the counter. "Keep the change." I noticed him slip my five into his pocket.

Dorcas finally exhaled, blowing us out the screen door on a cloud of smoke.

On the street, the train crowd had thinned, but people were still milling about. The row of brick shops across the street, which had been all touristy souvenirs, ice cream, and T-shirts, now offered a more sedate selection of dresses, hats for men, a bookstore, and a barbershop. People moved slower, strolling around, without that eager hunter-gatherer eye that had come to mark the shopping tourist. I was about to say, "of my era," but my mind just refused to go there.

John pulled a pack of unfiltered Luckies from his shirt pocket, expertly shook out one and held it out to me. I looked at it like he was offering me an unfiltered copperhead. He took that as a no, shrugged, and lit up with a big Zippo lighter.

"Okay, now tell me what's going on here, John. Please. I mean, I read science fiction when I was a kid – I can handle it. Heinlein, Asimov, Poul Anderson, all those guys. It's a classic story, right? Guy wakes up in a world he never made, has to figure out how to get back to – wherever. Whenever. But I gotta say, when you're in it and it's not just some story…. I am actually kind of freaking out here."

"Free what?"

"Freak. Ing. Out. John."

"'Freak' like in the circus? That's an interesting choice of words. Freak king out. Like you're going nuts, huh?"

"Yes, John, please. Let's take some time to discuss semantics. Really. You know what's going on, obviously. Tell me."

"Well, every now and then, one of you fellows – it's usually a fellow – is all-of-a-sudden standing in my shop. He's dressed odd, like…"

"Me. Go on, John."

"And he's agitated. Reminds me of some of the guys in the Army. After a battle, sometimes…."

"Me, John. Focus. I'm feeling very selfish right now for some reason. How'd I get here? And, more importantly, how do I get back?"

He turned and looked me in the eye. I swear his eyes twinkled. With just the trace of a smile, he said, "I believe you have to find the tooth."

"Find the tooth. Okay, it's an Indiana Jones kind of thing. I can do that. What tooth? Dinosaur? Saber-toothed tiger tooth? Where is it?"

"See, that's where it gets kinda tricky. It's not here. It hasn't happened yet."

"Uh huh, good. This is good. More of a Doctor Who type thing. I was a big fan when I was a kid. So, I have suddenly gone back sixty-some years in time because… what? I walked into your store? Fell down a tourist rabbit hole? And all I have to do to get back to my own sweet time and *everybody I know and love!* Okay, a little breath here. Would. Be. Good."

I took a deep, cleansing breath. John automatically breathed with me. We exhaled together, his exhalation smoke-tinged. "Whew," I said. "Okay. That was good. So, all I have to do is find a tooth, that doesn't exist yet, and presto, get back to my normal life. So, John, when will the tooth happen?"

"Doctor… who?"

16 Jerald Pope

"Yes, Doctor… oh, for god's sake. Now we're doing Abbot and Costello?"

"I oughta get back to the store. I love those guys. Who's on first? Now that's funny. Calm down, Odell; walk with me." We started back. The sun baked the brick buildings and streets, making the air feel like an oven set on low. "I don't know everything. Actually, I don't know much. But as you all come and go, I learn things, pick up stuff. There's a famous boy – a guitar player, seems like – who's gonna have a tooth pulled around on Broadway, in a dentist's office. You get that tooth, bring it back to my store, there's probably an incantation or something, and you're home."

"Now you're telling me…. Incantation? It's a little squirrelly sounding, but okay. We'll cross that bridge. Where's this dentist's office?"

"See, that's one of the problems. Your problems. It's not there yet."

"Oh? And when will it be there?"

"As best I understand it, 1973. You got twenty-five years."

John stood in the door of his shop as if that was all there was to say. He stubbed his cigarette out on the sidewalk and squinted at me, waiting.

"Okay, I'll bite. Twenty-five years?! That's not funny, John."

"No. No, it's not funny." He paused. "It is kind of amusing though, now that you mention it."

"Look. I have to find my fiancée. We're meeting her folks for dinner at that pizza place…" I pointed across the street to the garage of a car dealership. A man in coveralls was wrestling a wooden wheel off of a nineteen aught something pickup. "That *will be* right there. If I show up, suddenly twenty-five years older, there's gonna be questions. Plus, I got this little wedding thing in two days. Two days, John, not two days and twenty-five years."

"Well, actually, it is that long."

"No, no, no. I'm not gonna miss my wedding. This girl – Clarice – my bride, the love of my life, is depending on me to be there. She will be very, very upset if I'm not."

"I bet. Look. You're not supposed to know about this, but if you go around the corner, past the diner, there's a door between the hardware and the five and dime. There's a kind of, oh, club upstairs. Tell 'em I sent you, and do not get huffy with them. There's a guy hangs around there sometimes, name of… Shoot, what *is* his name? Anyway, they'll know who you're looking for. Tall guy, doesn't shave much, glasses, a little run down at the heels."

"Is he the tooth guy?"

John laughed and picked a little piece of tobacco off of his tongue. "No, no. Just find him, he knows more than I do about all this."

"Jesus H…"

"And if you'll take a little more advice, I'd watch that mouth. Here." He pulled a little purse out of his pocket and took out some crumpled bills. "Here's five dollars. Real money. That should get you by a week or so."

"I am not going to be here a week. Or twenty-five years."

"Okay. If you say so."

"I say so. Thanks for the five."

"Trade for your funny money. I'll keep it, might be worth something someday."

THE DANCE HALL

I rounded the corner from Cherry Street onto State Street. Sudsy was standing outside his shop, talking to a high-school-looking girl with wavy hair and saddle shoes. He stopped talking and blew smoke at me as I passed. I found the door, wooden with a pebbled glass window that said "Offices" on it. I pushed inside. A steep flight of stairs led up into a dark hall. As I walked up, a small thin man in a white suit and Panama hat hurried down. He seemed surprised to see me, started to say something, then ducked his head as he passed. At the bottom of the stairs he turned to look at me. We stared at each other for a moment, then he left.

At the top of the stairs, a dim light bulb hanging from the stamped tin ceiling bounced its yellowish light off the glossy cream-colored walls and the linoleum floor. The mirror at the top of the stairs gave the startling effect of someone walking up to meet you, until you realized it *was* you. After the bright sunlight on the street, it was taking my eyes a while to adjust. I saw a hall to the right, three more pebbled glass doors to the left, and a coatroom ahead, lit by an even dimmer bulb. No directory, no signs, nothing to indicate what sort of business or businesses occupied this upper floor. I could hear the clacking of a mechanical typewriter and the whisper of a radio down the hall.

I stepped into the coatroom, which had no coats, just rows of hooks on three of the walls. In the middle of the wall opposite me was a wooden door with a small round peephole at eye level. "You've got to be kidding," I muttered. I hadn't seen any other people since the little man on the stairs. I knocked on the door.

Nothing. I tried to look through the peephole, but it was blocked on the other side by a metal plug. I thought I heard music faintly playing inside. I knocked again, trying the shave-and-a-haircut rhythm I'd seen in old black and white gangster movies. Still getting no response, I pushed my finger through the peephole to see if I could move the plug. It swung up and back, and there was a big eye, blinking at me. It didn't seem like a happy eye.

"Ow! You poked my eye!" a deep, unhappy voice said.

"Sorry. Listen, can I come in? Are you open?"

"No, you can't. Not unless….Well, who sent you?"

"John, the guy at the Time Shop? He told me I should come up here."

"Come on in, the door's open. What you sneaking around out there for, anyway?"

"Oh." I pushed the door open to find a large, low-ceilinged, open space. Tiny tables, each flanked by two chairs, sat around the walls on a low raised platform. A tiny bandstand was at the far end, flanked by two windows covered with heavy dark drapery. They leaked a dirty brown light which didn't penetrate very far into the room. A jukebox, lit up like an old fashioned Christmas tree, sat next to the bandstand, playing a whiny fiddle song. A bar to my left had a couple of people sitting at it, otherwise the place was empty. The room was dimly lit by eight kitchen light fixtures spread around the ceiling, interspersed with eight slowly turning ceiling fans.

A very large man in overalls stood in front of me, his hand over his right eye. He must have been over six and a half feet tall, large in every way, but the biggest thing about him was his belly, which strained the front of his overalls. He was glowering at me, blocking my way.

"You poked my eye."

"I'm sorry."

"Who is it, Tiny?" A raspy female voice called from the bar. The big guy's name was "Tiny."

"He poked my eye," Tiny said. He was obviously the kind of guy who held on to a grudge.

"I told you not to use that peep thing. When you gonna learn? Come on over, Mister."

Tiny grudgingly stepped aside and I sidled by him. If he was the tall, down-at-the-heels guy I was supposed to see, I'd really gotten off on the wrong foot. I thought I'd let him cool off a bit. I patted his arm, very gently. "I didn't mean... Sorry about your eye." I went over to the bar.

It wasn't a well stocked bar. Three half-empty bottles sat on the back shelf and a large metal, coffin-shaped box crouched on the floor. I recognized it as an old-fashioned soda cooler, the kind you filled with ice and fished around in the freezing water until you found the bottle you were looking for. Matching hula dancers with lampshades for skirts stood on either end of the worn wooden bar, marginally brightening it. The bartender wore a dark fedora with an unlit cigarette jammed in the corner of his mouth. He had a newspaper spread out on the bar, catching the light from under one of the hula girls' skirts. He stared at me briefly, then went back to his paper.

At the other end of the bar sat the woman. She was surprisingly young for a barfly, if that's what she was. She had blond hair that curled out from her head in a bold steel-wool-looking perm. She was wearing a short-sleeved white blouse and red earrings that matched her necklace. Her cigarette burned in an ashtray on the bar. The ashtray was also a hula girl. I was obviously in a proto-tiki bar. Her face, from what I could tell in the dim light, was friendly. Cute, in a slightly buck-toothed sort of way. She had a picture magazine opened in front of her. Everyone was reading. Apparently it was a literary proto-tiki bar. Then I noticed the man, awkwardly lying face down in her lap.

She saw me looking at him. "Hey," she said, gently shaking his head. "Mister Mayor. Rise and shine."

The man mumbled into her skirt. She smiled at me in a friendly way that definitely made her seem cuter. "He's a very busy man. Very important. He comes in sometimes to get away from all the important things he has to do. You know, take a break."

"Hey, who am I to judge?"

"You're not nobody. This here's the mayor." Okay, so not so friendly. "If you come in here to judge people, 'specially important upright people, you surely come in the wrong place."

The mayor reared up and flopped his arms on the bar. He rested his head on them and turned a bleary eye toward me. "Judge?" he said, then collapsed again.

"Far be it from me to… I just came in here looking for someone." I turned to the bartender. "Can I get a beer?"

Without looking up from his paper, the bartender said, "This here's a dry town, Judge. We don't serve liquor."

"Yeah, I don't want liquor, which I see you don't have, just a beer."

"Dry town, no beer. Doctor Pepper, RC, Co'cola. Might have a Cheerwine."

"Oh for Pete's sake, Pete," the woman said. "Give the Judge here a beer."

The bartender shrugged, ambled over to the cooler, raised the lid and fished around in the ice water, finally pulled out a brown bottle. The paper label slid off the bottle as he wiped it off, falling back into the cooler. He popped the lid with an opener attached to the side of the cooler and set the dripping bottle on the bar. "Fifty cents, Judge."

"Pete!" the woman said. "It's a quarter, Mister."

I laid one of my dollar bills on the bar. "Keep the change," I said. Pete raised an eyebrow, but pocketed the money.

"Hey, big spender." The girl stuck out her hand. "My name's Dixie. Glad to meetcha."

"Bi'shpenders," the mayor muttered into his arm.

"Hi, Dixie. Can I buy you a beer?"

"Why not? Gimme a beer, Pete." I started to pull out another dollar, but Dixie put her hand on my arm. "And take it out of the Judge's dollar."

"That's my tip, Dixie,"

"Oh, you wanna tip? I got a tip for you, soldier," she said, lowering her head and staring at him from under her steely bangs. These two obviously had history.

"Dammit, Dix, you know I'm Navy. Don't call me 'soldier.'"

"I know, I know. Pacific theater, tin-can destroyers, blahdy blahdy blah." She puckered her lips and blew him a little kiss. With her slightly protruding teeth, it really was charming.

"How 'bout you, Judge? How'd you spend the War?"

I took a pull on my beer. It was cold and tasted good and I needed some time. If this was 1948, World War Two had only been over for, what? Three years. It was still a Big Deal in my time, so it would be a Very Big Deal in this one. Quite a Very Big Deal. For me to say I'd never been in the military would not endear me to these people. They'd been through a lot – saved the world, Greatest Generation. Non-participants need not apply. The only honorable thing to do was to lie.

"Well, you know. Army, First Division."

"Uh," Pete said. "Normandy, eh?"

"No, I missed that one. But after, right after."

"Yeah, France, Germany; tough row to hoe. Here." He handed me back the dollar. "This one's on me, GI."

Okay, now I felt bad – worse than a coward who didn't fight. Pete, for all his surliness, had done his duty. How could I explain 9-11 to these folks? The volunteer army? Iraq, the wrong war? And our ten years fooling around in Afghanistan. That's six years longer than they had taken to whip both the Germans and the Japanese at the same time; two very big, very scary, real armies. I laid the dollar on the bar.

"Let me return the favor, sailor. Have one on me."

"Don't mind if I do," Pete said, turning and taking one of the unlabeled bottles off the shelf. He poured himself a shot of a white liquor and knocked it back. "Ahh. That'll put hair on your chest!"

Dixie raised her bottle. "Here's to the boys."

"Me too!" the mayor pounded weakly on the bar, not lifting his head. "I'm hairy!" Pete poured him a shot and set it in front of him. The mayor pulled the glass to him and lapped the contents like a dog, still keeping his head securely on the bar. "To our boysh," he slurred and belched a foul, invisible cloud that rolled down the bar. The three of us who were upright leaned smartly back to let it pass.

"Gee, time for you to be gettin' back to work, Mister Mayor," Dixie said. "Duty calls."

"Nahmokay, Dix."

"Tiny, you wanna help the mayor back to his office?"

Tiny, who had been sulking in the corner by the door during all this, shambled toward us.

"Um, Tiny," I said. "Before you go, John said there was a guy, hangs out here, might help me out. Tall guy, uh, casually dressed, glasses. Do you wear glasses?"

"Glasses? If I'd a had glasses, you wouldn'ta poked my eye. Right?"

"Forget it, Tiny," Dixie said. "Just haul the mayor outa here, and don't let him puke on the stairs again."

Tiny picked the mayor up under the arms and carried him, not ungently, out the door. Pete wiped the spilled booze, drool and tears from where the mayor had been lying, which prompted Dixie to hold up her skirt to see what liquid damage the mayor had done there.

"He's got a lot on his mind, these days. We're really lucky to have him."

"I see," I said.

"Tiny's not the fellah you're lookin for. There's another one, tall, but not as big as Tiny. He wears these funny lookin' glasses. Talks with John a lot. Dale Ray… something."

"Dale Ray Something. Does he have another last name?"

"Yeah, see, we ain't much for last names around here."

"Uh huh, I'm getting that. Has he been around? Will he be in today? I kind of need to talk to him."

Dixie took a thoughtful sip of her beer. I was aware how aware she was of the way her red painted lips negotiated the beer bottle. She was obviously a professional beer drinker. "Hey, Pete. Seen ole Dale Ray lately?"

"Nah, he's in jail, remember? Was hollerin' in the street again. Public drunk."

"Again? That boy has got the troubles, I tell you."

"Okay, good. Dale Ray Something in the jail. Now we're getting somewhere. Where can I find the jail?"

"Up the street, right out front, about two blocks left. Next to the fire station is City Hall. Jail's in the basement."

"Good deal. Thanks for the info, Dixie. It's been a pleasure. Thanks for the beer, Pete."

"Judge."

"Well, good luck," Dixie stood. She was short, maybe five-three, five-four. "Tell Dale Ray we said hey. Maybe we'll see you again – what was your name? I didn't get it."

"Probably you won't. I have an important, um, engagement somewhere else. But the name is Odell. Odell Lutz."

"Well, Odell Odell Lutz, it's sure been nice to meet you. If you do hang around – if you need anything, anything at all, you know where to find me."

"No, it's just Odell, not… Yes, I do. You all take care, now." I left them where I'd found them, leaning on the bar in the dance hall. I went through the dim hallways and down the stairs to the street. It was still hot, and still fairly busy. The beer had calmed the static of fear in my chest, but I could feel it begin to reassert itself. I hurried down the street, past the café where Sudsy was still outside, talking to a different girl this time. He didn't bother to blow smoke at me as I passed. I was starting to fit in. I really didn't want that. I crossed Cherry Street and headed up the block to City Hall.

The Elvis Tooth 29

30 Jerald Pope

JAIL

The fire station and the city hall hugged each other like two old spinster sisters. Two-story brick buildings, they radiated that modest elegance that many small town public buildings of bygone eras had; an elegance that faded in the Fifties and was violently crushed in the Sixties and Seventies. I went up the steps to City Hall. A Western Union telegraph office occupied the right, with a town office on the left. I popped my head in the town office.

"I'm looking for the jail?"

A gray-haired lady in a blue flowered dress looked up from behind the counter. "Police department, stairs on the left, Sugar. Down, not up."

I went down the stairs to the little police station. A desk with two white-globed lamps on either side sat in a small room with four unmarked doors. The one at the far end was obviously the door to the outside. Next to it a large bulletin board was covered with wanted posters and notices for lost cats.

"Hello?" I called. "Anyone around?"
Silence for a moment, then a muffled voice behind one of the doors coughed and said, "in here." I opened the door and saw a large cage made of flat metal bands sitting in the middle of the

room. Inside were two metal bunk-beds and a metal table with two beat up wooden stools beside it. A pack of cigarettes and some worn out playing cards lay on the table.

Two men were inside the cell. One lay on a lower bunk, a hat over his face, asleep. The other draped his arms on the bars facing me. He was dark complexioned, lanky, wearing worn-out khaki pants and shirt and a beat-up brown fedora. He had what looked like a week's growth of what would someday be an admirable beard and the most bloodshot eyes I'd ever seen. He was the very picture of a small town drunk. "Hey," he said.

"Are you Dale Ray?"

"Might be."

"Do you wear glasses? Funny looking glasses."

He pulled a pair of round, tortoise-shell glasses out of his shirt pocket. One lens was shattered. "Who wants to know?"

"John, over at the Time Shop, said I should talk to you."

"Huh. How'd you find me here?"

"Dixie, Pete."

"Okay. So, what do you want? I'm kinda busy."

"Yeah, I see. Where's the policeman – men?"

"He's got stuff to do. Leaves me in charge when he goes out. We don't get a lot of excitement around here. Dogs, drunks, speeding tickets."

"Well, if you're working here, how come you're in the...."

"Tank? Drunk and disorderly. It happens, sometimes. Judge gave me four days. I'm in and out so much, Pug Morgan kind of made me an unofficial deputy."

"Pug Morgan's the police chief?"

"Yeah, we got a police chief *and* a policeman."

"Interesting. So, Dale Ray, I got a problem I'm hoping you can help me with. See, I'm not from around here."

"I figured. 'Tourist' written all over you."

"And I was in the Time Shop, just sort of looking around, and – suddenly – it was 1948."

Dale Ray jerked like he'd stuck his finger in an electrical socket. He stood up straight and the bleary-eyed hangover look faded from his eyes. He shot a glance at the man lying in the bunk. He waved me closer. "What year?" he whispered.

"Twenty thirteen. How do you…?"

"Wow, cool," he said. "The future. I'm from '91. So we survived the millennium, eh?"

I looked around for a chair, saw one against the wall and sat down heavily. "You… you time-traveled too?"

"Yep, I've been here five years, most of the War. That was rough, let me tell you. No papers, no history, I coulda been a spy, or they coulda thought I was."

"Jeez. How'd you keep from getting caught?"

"John, and a couple of others. You'll meet them, eventually."

"No, no, I don't *want* to meet them eventually. I want to get back to my own...." I swallowed hard. I didn't want to even put it into words. "My own time. I'm getting married in, like forty-eight hours. I have to meet my fiancée. Her parents are here with us. They're all going to be really upset when – *if* – I don't show up."

"Yeah, well."

"Five years! You've been here five years? Did you even try to get back?"

"Okay, keep your voice down. Ole Carl here would love to spread the rumor I was a spaceman or something. I kind of tried, for a while. Only a couple of days, really. Then I realized, I like it here. So I sort of stayed."

"*Sort of* stayed? Brother, you stayed."

"Like I say, I like it here. Everything is so much… fresher, more innocent. People, even the crooks and politicians, have a – I don't know – naïve hopefulness that was totally lacking in our time. At least in anyone over the age of six. The air is cleaner here, the food is tastier, the jokes are funnier. There're no cell phones, TVs, computers, or baseball strikes. Plus I know a lot of stuff that's gonna happen, so I make a decent living betting on things – baseball, politics, current events."

"But you're a drunk. In jail."

"Yeah, but I'm a happy drunk. And it's *my* jail."

"Okay. But I'm not happy. I want to go home to my own time, my own people."

"You're crazy. You oughta try it for a while, anyway."

"No thanks. I wanna go back. John said you know something."

"Absolutely. Listen. In 1976, Elvis Presley will come through Black Mountain on his way to play a concert in Asheville. He'll have a bad toothache. Remember, this is the Seventies Fat Elvis – probably rotted his teeth with fried banana sandwiches. His bus will pull off Highway 70; Scotty, his guitar player, will get out and ask an old lady for directions. They'll pull the bus around on Broadway, just down from the drugstore on the corner, and Elvis will go upstairs to Dr. James Love's office. Dr. Love will have a patient leave the chair—he's a big Elvis fan. Love, not the patient—slot Elvis in there and pull a tooth – a lower back molar with a gold crown, I believe. When the local paper interviews Dr. Love about the event, he won't be able to locate the tooth, which would have been a choice piece of memorabilia."

"And you're telling me all this because…?"

"The tooth is a key. You need it to get back to your time. You get it, take it back to Pellom's, which is obviously your gate, and presto change-o, you're there."
"How do you know this?"

"Common knowledge."

"Yeah? Among who?"

"Timers, the people who got here the way we did."

"And how do I get to 1976?"

"I have no idea."

"Dammit!" I banged my head against the bars.

"Keep it down, Spaceman, keep it down," Carl grumbled from his bunk and rolled over.

"But I know someone who does know," Dale Ray said. "Oh, look. Pug's back with the new police car. Oh boy, it's a Mercury!"

A shiny new black and white police cruiser with a cherry on top was crunching into the gravel lot from the alley behind the jail.

"Wow. Now who is this guy who knows about Elvis?"

"You know, you oughta go. Pug doesn't like me having visitors when I'm on duty. Come back tonight after midnight. Come in this downstairs door, it'll be open."

"But…"

"Really, go on. Scoot. Twelve o'clock."

Pug Morgan, a barrel-chested man in a blue uniform with a red face, came whistling in the door. "Hey, Dale Ray, come see the new…oh." He stopped, seeing me and put on his cop face. "What are you doing in here? This is off limits."

"Yeah. Hi. I was just looking for the telegraph office. This kind gentleman told me I had to go upstairs."

"That's right. It's the one on the left as you're looking out."

"Can't miss it," Dale Ray added, helpfully.

I tried to catch Dale Ray's eye one last time, but he was involved with Pug Morgan opening the cell so that he and Carl could come out and admire the new car. I went back up the stairs. A sign on the Western Union office said Ellen would be right back. The official, Western Union clock said four thirty. I had seven and a half hours to kill. As I thought of the phrase, "killing time," the lump returned to my throat.

A train whistled in the distance. I wandered down the hill behind city hall to watch the train come in. It was a pleasant little knoll, reclaiming what had recently been a burned down building. A boy was mowing it with what would someday be an old-fashioned rotary mower. The dandelions and clover fell with each push. The kid was actually whistling as if he enjoyed the work. The green mountains surrounding the town glowed with that particular hot summer shimmer. White, sheep-like clouds grazed across the sky. A little breeze wafted up the hill to cool my face.

I could feel myself slipping, against my will, into the easy-going rhythm of this place and time. No rush, no crushing worry, a bright sun-shiny day to swing in like a backyard hammock. A person could lay back, drink a lemonade, and just wait for something interesting to come along.

38 Jerald Pope

THE DEPOT

All this Boys Life nostalgia was making my teeth hurt. I picked up my pace as the train pulled into the station. Several 1920s' style pickups were backed up on the east side of the station. An actual buckboard wagon with a mule hitched to it sat among the pickups, looking not at all out of place. A few people drifted up as the train gave a big steamy sigh and eased to a stop. I sat on a bench across from the station to watch the show.

Immediately, black porters in starched white jackets and red caps jumped down from the three passenger cars, set steps in front of the doors, and stood by at a relaxed attention. There was a pause, then people started dribbling out in ones and twos. It was so different from the push and crunch when a twenty-first century public conveyance, say an airplane pulled up to the terminal; people jumping up, ignoring the order to wait until the plane stopped moving, grabbing their stuff from the overhead bins and lining up in the tiny aisle to wait, wait, inching slowly forward until they finally spurt through the door to race away, like a bursting aneurism.

I noticed two gawky teenage boys in slacks and short-sleeved shirts. One of them wore a brown slouch hat with a piece of paper stuck in the brim, the other was carrying an old bellows camera tied around his neck with a string. They were scanning the windows of the three cars, looking for someone. One of them gave a shout and they both converged on the middle car.

An attractive young redhead in a light green summer suit, spectator pumps and a hat and gloves paused in the door, and the two boys stood at her feet, talking earnestly. She seemed confused, then smiled prettily. She struck an awkward glamour pose and the boy with the camera took her picture. She went through several more poses, more coltish than seductive, as the cameraman snapped away, the porter waiting patiently and smiling broadly. When she descended from the train, the boy with the hat took her aside, whipped out a pad and pencil, and conducted a short, intense interview. The boy tipped his hat, the girl smiled, the cameraman grabbed one last shot, and she went on her way.

The boys went back to search the train, but by now, everyone who was getting off had done so. Smiling and comparing notes, they crossed the street near where I sat. The one in the hat glanced at me, glanced again and changed direction, coming over to me. When he got close, I saw the paper stuck in his brim said "press."

"Hey, Mister, what kind of shoes are those?" he asked, pointing at my feet. I was wearing my exploring shoes, low-topped hikers with slots for breathing and orange laces. I also had on

jeans and a striped polo shirt. Not too out of synch with the local attire. Oh, and the shoes were lime green camo.
"Experimental military model, son. I was testing them up at White Sands. They let me have them when we were done."

"Those are nutty," the one with the camera said.

"Sorry, you can't take their picture. Still, you know, classified. Hush hush."

"Aw, there's no film in this thing. I don't even think it would work if I *did* have film."

"But weren't you just taking that young lady's picture? The one on the train?"

The boys looked at each other and grinned. The cameraman handed me the camera to inspect. "She *thought* I was taking her picture. See, we figured out this little racket...."

"It was my idea," the reporter said. "We come down to meet the trains; look for pretty girls who are coming to town, and pretend to interview them for the Black Mountain paper."

"Which there ain't any," interrupted the photographer.

"Yeah, but they don't know that. We tell 'em we're doing a special story, talking to pretty girls, putting their picture in the paper."

"I snap a bunch of pictures while they pose for us. They're always flattered."

"And I interview them. Get their name, where they're from, how long they're gonna be here, where they're staying...."

"We promise to bring them by some copies of the pictures, that's why we need their local address. But...."

"Like this girl here," the reporter referred to his notes. "Marcy Taylor. Oklahoma girl. She's staying up in Montreat with her grandparents. She'll be here two weeks."

"Tomorrow, we'll go up there, all hang-dog and apologetic. Say, gee, the pictures didn't come out."

"Yeah, bad film or something. We can't run the story, of course; and we got no pictures to give her. We feel terrible."

"If only there were some way we could make it up to her."

The boys snapped their fingers at the same time. The reporter said. "You know, there just happens to be a barn dance tonight. It's not as good as getting your picture in the paper, but we'd be glad to take you dancing."

"As a way of apologizing for the mess up."

The two boys looked at each other, beaming.

"And how does it work, this scheme of yours?" I asked.

"Real good," they said in unison.

"We've met some mighty pretty girls," said the photographer, almost giggling.

"And a girl will go out with two strange boys?"

"We always ask if they've got a friend or a sister."

"And we meet their folks."

"And most people know our families."

"It seems like the local girls would keep a couple of Romeos like you two busy."

"Oh, Black Mountain girls," the reporter almost spat. "They're too stuck-up."

"Plus, they know us too well," said the other.

"But you score pretty good with the out-of-towners?"

"Yes sir, we do all right," grinned the photographer. "Bill here has had seven dates already this summer. Two with the same girl."

"And Buddy got a kiss last year!" They both blushed at this information, but were obviously bursting with pride.

"My, you boys are *bad*!" I laughed.

Suddenly the boys looked serious, even a little offended.

"No, sir, we're not," Bill, the reporter said. 'We'd never do anything to spoil a girl's reputation."

"We're just having fun," frowned Buddy, the photographer.

"I know you are, boys," I said, backtracking. "I was just pulling your leg. Legs."

"Well, we gotta get going," said Buddy, smiling again. "Gotta get this film developed!"

They shook my hand, their optimistic mood restored, and headed off down the street. Obviously the debauched world of the fifties was still safely around the corner- at least in this little town. I wondered what Bill and Buddy would make of teenagers in the twenty-first century, with their hook-ups and dirty dancing at the high school prom. They were definitely squares by the standards of my time. But I had to admit, they were charming squares.

It came to me that I had just had another little taste of what Dale Ray was talking about. I could sense the siren charms of a simpler, kinder, Norman-Rockwellian age calling, "Stay, stay."

"No!" I shouted loudly in my inner voice. "I will not stay! I will not sit! I will not roll over!" I stood up suddenly from the bench, scaring a squirrel that had been timidly approaching, apparently mistaking me for one of those aimless do-littles who sat around feeding squirrels. I barked at it and it raced crazily across the street. If there'd been any traffic, it would have been squirrel-burger, but of course there wasn't.

I checked my phone. Only six short hours until my rendezvous with Dale Ray. Just for fun, I tried making a call to my wife's cell. It didn't work. I would have been surprised if it did, but then, this day was one big surprise. I was glad the clock part of the phone worked. Although, come to think of it, was it *now* time, *then* time, or *future* time? Good, now I had something else to worry about. I decided to call it "now" and let that one go. For now.

I walked down Sutton Avenue, past the train station, now practically deserted in the late afternoon heat. Peering in the windows, I could see the stationmaster, or whatever he was, slumped on a bench in the waiting room, napping. It was clean, bright, and otherwise empty. Against the outside wall was a little newsstand selling *Look, Life, Colliers, Photoplay* and a variety of newspapers. I idly picked up the *Charlotte Observer* to see what the big news was. A guy named Alger Hiss was testifying before Congress; heard of him. Babe Ruth died; heard of him. A new game called Scrabble was sweeping the country; heard of that. So things weren't totally strange. I mean, at least I wasn't on Mars.

"That'd be a nickel, Mister," a little voice said from somewhere. I looked around. Next to the newsstand, a young kid sat in the shade, his back against the wall, a wooden box in front of him. "How about a shine while you're…" He stopped when he saw my shoes. He lifted his cap and scratched his head. "Wow. What kinda shoes you got there?"

"Kind of hiking shoes." Not exactly a lie, but it was coming easier. "They're the latest thing up North."

"Those are some crazy colors for a growed man to be wearing."

"Well, you know. It's a Northern thing."

"I sure hope I don't see any more of 'em. Put me outa business."

"Oh, I think you got a few years before they get down here. You sell papers and shine shoes?"

"Nah, Mister Papadopolis, runs the paper stand, went home for supper. We take turns watchin' each other's business. No business anyway if there ain't no train. You want that paper? It's still a nickel."

"No, I think I'll pass." I laid the paper down. "You have a nice day, okay?"

"That's a silly thing to say. Day's almost done."

"Okay. Well, I'll see you around, then, maybe."

THE BUS STATION

I thought I would drop in on John Pellom, see what else he could tell me. Maybe he knew this Dale Ray character and could give me some insight. As I crossed Sutton, a big aluminum whale turned in front of me onto Cherry Street. A streamlined Greyhound bus, its every line crying "modern" in the most retro fashion. Except "retro" hadn't been invented yet.

I vaguely remembered a useless college class on "the Invention of the Modern" or some such silliness. The fifties were coming, when America would embrace the idea of the Future. Sincerely try to become the world of the Jetsons – fins, rockets, parabolas, and plastic. Only after that grand effort started to crumble in the late Sixties would we start picking and choosing certain elements of it to celebrate. Thus, Retro. I recalled that the class hadn't been entirely useless – there was that cute redheaded art major. Who became my first wife. Okay, it was useless after all.

I followed the bus up the hill to the little bus station. I noticed the "newspapermen" weren't checking the new bus arrivals for a human interest story. I had no idea how bus riding fit into 1940s American class structure. A couple of cars were parked along the street, obviously waiting for friends or family arriving on the bus.

The bus station was just a storefront, no different than the others on that side of the street except for the Greyhound painted on the windows and a white globe light hanging over the main door. A smaller door to the right had the word "colored" lettered on it. I peeked in and saw that both doors opened into the same room. Toward the back was a low fence like you'd see in a court-room; another "colored" sign hung above it. There were what looked to be the exact same benches and chairs on both sides of the fence. This is what used to be accepted as normal in America. Yikes.

The bus had its windows open to the late afternoon heat. Universal air-conditioning was still a decade away. I could see passengers fanning themselves – with actual paper fans – waiting for the bus to start moving again. A soldier in khaki got off the bus, his face lit up as he waved at someone, then he ran to get into a car parked across the street.

After a moment, an African-American family of four climbed down and gathered up a clutch of tired-looking suitcases as the driver pulled them from under the bus. They gathered up their luggage and stumbled up the street. I followed them for a bit, then, as the little girl dropped one of the three bags she was carrying for the second time, decided to help out. Shoot, I apparently had the time.

"Excuse me, folks. Can I lend a hand?"

The father turned around with relief on his face, but when he saw me he stiffened up. "No, sir, thank-you-kindly. We're doin' just fine."

Confused, I looked at his sweating wife, gangly daughter, and pint-sized son, all over-loaded with different sized and colored cases. "No, come on, I got nothing to do. I'd be glad to help."

The family stared tensely at the father, waiting for his decision. He looked around the street, either for help or judgment. "I do appreciate it, sir. But I just don't think it'd be right, a white man carryin' for black folk."

"Oh, right," I said. And he was right, and it was the segregated South. But they were also in need of help, and it was still hot. I noticed that they had walked right by a cab that was waiting by the bus station. "Well, where I come from, that's not such a big deal."

"Are you from France?" the girl asked.

"No, sugar, but I am from pretty far away. Most people there look at things differently than they do around here. And you all look like you could use a little help. So, I'll risk it."

I reached to take a bag from the wife, but she took a half step back and shook her head. "Ain't no risk for *you*, mister," she said. "The risk is all on us."

"Angela…" her husband cautioned.

She was right. I was a stranger in a strange land: I didn't know the whole score. The sylvan Mayberry haze that enveloped this little-town-that-time-would-forget didn't cast its golden net for everybody. It was America. It was the South. It was 1948. "You're right, Ma'am," I apologized. "I didn't mean to cause you folks trouble."

The adults visibly relaxed, but the kids, especially the little boy, looked hot and disappointed. "Aw, mama," he whined.

She wiped the sweat from his brow and contemplated her son for a moment. "You know," she said. "If we was to leave, oh, say four of these bags on the sidewalk here. By this bench. Just accidental like. And then walk off. And if someone – some stranger – was to come along and pick them up, and just happen to be walkin' the same direction as us. Not *with* us, you understand. And when we got up to where we're 'sposed to meet Uncle Nate, and that someone just happened to put the bags down by where we was standin'. Well, that'd be just a sort of amazing coincidence, now wouldn't it?"

The boy and girl looked hopefully at their father who heaved an exasperated sigh and scratched his head under his hat.

"Angela…." he started, but stopped when she raised an eyebrow at him. "You'ns sit down on that bench, rest your feet," he said to the kids, who obeyed immediately. "We're gonna take just a minute, catch our breath, then we got to be gettin' up to where Uncle Nate's pickin' us up. That'd be the corner of State and Broadway."

The wife sat beside them and removed one of her gloves, then took out a lace-trimmed hanky. She wiped the girl's brow, then the boy's, then her own. The big silver bus revved its diesel engine and chugged up the hill past us. We all struck awkward, innocent poses.

"It's been a long trip from Aunt Johnnie's, but we're almost home, children," the man said, after the bus had turned the corner. "Let's go, and be careful to only take your one bag, Ruby. You too, Marvin."

The kids stood up, each taking the heaviest bag they were carrying. Marvin reached up and took a bag from his mother, who smiled gratefully at him. They left four bags by the bench as they walked away, the man nodding to me. I sat on the bench to give them a decent head start. It was an odd situation; we were all acting like bad secret agents. Or I could be a notorious luggage thief and there'd be nothing they could do about it. They were trusting a stranger who had intruded in their lives, perhaps causing them at the least, discomfort, at the most, real danger. I picked up the bags, which were heavier than they looked, and followed them up the street.

John was standing in front of the Time Shop, smoking. "I saw that," he said, then raised an eyebrow. I just nodded, sweating under my load, and headed on up the street.

I turned the corner onto State and saw the family turning the corner down Broadway, the boy leaning back to see if I was coming. I hurried to catch up. Around the corner, past the Rexall drug store, an old open touring car from the Twenties sat, chugging rhythmically. The man and another fellow about his age were loading the suitcases on a rack on the back. I set my bags down next to theirs and went on down the street. "Thanks, Mister," the man said.

"Daddy, it's just like that picture we saw," Marvin was saying as I walked away. "Remember, with the German spy and the dancer? Daddy, am I supposed to be the spy or the dancer?"

52 Jerald Pope

AVENA'S BOWLING ALLEY

All the businesses on Broadway were closed, but one. On the corner and across the street, a one-story wooden building was well-lit from within. I crossed over and read the windows: Avena's Bowling Alley. Well, that hadn't survived to the twenty-first century! In my time, it was a labyrinthian furniture store, taking up the whole block. "In my time!" The very words made the tightness rise in my chest again. I needed to knock something down with much noise and fury. I needed to bowl.

I opened the ubiquitous screen door and entered. Four lanes and no automation – this was a prehistoric bowling alley. At the far end, a bench ran along the wall with two young boys sitting on it. A single bowler danced up to the line and threw the ball, which wasn't the big, satisfying twenty pounder of *Bowling for Dollars* fame, but smaller, about the size of a croquet ball, and with no finger-holes. When it knocked down the pins, which were also smaller, one of the boys scurried out and cleared away the dead soldiers. Caveman bowling. A dusty chalkboard on the wall had room for up to eight bowlers to mark their scores.

A small counter ran across the front of the joint and about ten customers, all men, were hanging around, watching the solo bowler. Nine of them were smoking. Behind the counter was a grill where a swarthy man with a waxed moustache and a bowler hat was cooking a hamburger, his cigarette occasionally sprinkling the meat with ashes. I slid into a space at the counter; there weren't any seats. "How much for a game?" I asked.

"Quarter," said the man next to me.

"Sounds reasonable. I'll have a game and a beer, please."

My neighbor laughed and coughed simultaneously. "What part of Yankee-land are you from, pal? This is a dry…"

"Town," I finished for him. "Right, I forgot."

"I was goin' to say 'county,' but town'll do. You want some competition?"

"What I really want is a beer, but I guess I could take you on."

"Well sir. It wouldn't be me. It'd be her." And he nodded toward a woman who was standing on the sidewalk at a service window that opened into the bar. The mustachioed man had wrapped the hamburger in paper and was handing it through the window to the woman. "Hey, Count. Tell Betty she's got a game."

The cook gave us a nod and leaned through the window to talk to the woman. She stood there, munching her burger, then shrugged and came around the corner to come inside. She was an old woman, short, with tight ringlets of white hair around her head. The hair was sparse enough to show lots of scalp. Her cheeks were rouged orange, and her mouth, which looked like she'd had a long and successful career sucking lemons, was caked with red lipstick that made no real attempt to follow the outline of her lips. Her white blouse was sprinkled with the remains of her hamburger, as well as traces of hamburgers past. She wore a wrinkled skirt that might once have been brown, beige stockings that were rolled to just below her knees, and run-down brown oxfords. "You bowl?" she said.

"Never did this version – what's it called?"

"Duck Pin," she said. "It's the game Rip Van Winkle was playing when he fell asleep for twenty years. I was a schoolteacher for twenty years, too. My name is Betty Bickerson."

Gritch gritch. I was hearing this odd sound, like a wooden South American cricket toy. I looked around the room; most of the patrons were watching us with big encouraging smiles on their faces. This set up with Betty was obviously an old gag. "Teacher, eh?"

"Yep. History, mostly." *Gritch gritch.* "That's how come I know all about Rip Van Winkle." *Gritch gritch.* "The game's the same as ten-pin, except where it's different. Try to knock 'em all down." *Gritch.* "You get three bowls per frame instead of two. Three hundred's a perfect game." *Gritch gritch gritch.* "I have bowled a 300 game, just so's you know."*Gritch gritch.*

The sound, which was by far the loudest noise in the room, was coming from Betty's mouth. She was apparently grinding her teeth, and she apparently had some hellacious false choppers in there. She was also apparently unaware of how loud the noise was.

"So, Betty Bickerson, are those new teeth?" I asked. I thought if I made her self-conscious, it might throw her off her game – give me a little edge.

"Nope. These are my Sunday teeth." *Gritch gritch.* "I only wear them on Sunday." *Gritch.* "I'm from Ohio, too. But I mostly taught in St. Louis." *Gritch gritch gritch.*

"I see. But isn't today Saturday?"

"Yep. You want me to go first, show you how it's done?" *Gritch?*

"Sure. Is it customary to place a little friendly wager on the game?"

She turned, looked at the peanut gallery and wiggled her eyebrows at them. It was a totally bizarre gesture. "I guess I could afford to lose, say, *gritch gritch,* a dollar?"

I pulled a bill out of my pocket and put it on the counter. Immediately, six of the hangers-out slapped their own dollars on mine. "I'll take a little piece of that. Guess I could risk a buck. I'm in. Me too."

"Hey, I can't cover you all."

"Tell you what," one of them said. "We kinda like you, so we'll give you two to one."

"I appreciate that, fellows. So, Miz Bickerson, show me how this game works."

She picked up one of the balls, cupped it underhanded, stood in the lane, took three surprisingly quick steps for an old lady, and let fly. The ball didn't roll down the lane, or do the kind of skidding backspin associated with real bowling. I don't know how it's supposed to be done, but in Betty Bickerson's game, the ball skipped once and plowed into the pins. She left the nine pin standing on her first roll – or throw.

She started out strong, telling me how she'd learned to play when she worked for the Army Air Force in Buffalo during the war. She said she was a WAC. I bit my tongue.

But I was pitcher for a softball team back home and, though the ball was three times as heavy, I soon got the hang of it. We were neck and neck by the ninth frame and most of the gang had fallen silent. Their six dollars were on the line. One guy though was kibitzing like Bugs Bunny at a dog race. He was laying out these groaners that were getting zero response from the crowd, but he just kept on.

"Man, if you was a farmer, Betty'd clean your plow. Uh huh.

"I ain't seen a man throw a ball like that since I was in kindygarden. And that man was a *girl*! Surely was.

"Wait a minute, wait a minute, let me go home and bring my ole dog up here. He's lazy, but I want to show him lazy! Yes I do."

"Shut up, Choogy," one of the bettors finally said. "Let the man bowl." I don't think Choogy actually had any money riding on the game. But Choogy looked at the guy like he'd called him the funniest thing since banana peels.

"I know!" he said.

The cook leaned across the counter and tapped the kibitzer on the shoulder. "You know what your problem is, Choogy? You think you're the cat's meow, but you ain't."

"What d'ya mean, Count?" Choogy had a big grin, but there was a nervous edge to it.

"In a nutshell, Choogy, and I been meaning to tell you this for a couple years now, you just ain't that funny."

Choogy stared hard at the Count, his grin fading. He started to say something, looked around at his friends, who were nodding like a collection of motley hillbilly bobbleheads, and shut up.

Everyone in the place but me was now smoking meditatively. Betty squinted through the smoke from a lipstick-stained cigarette clinched firmly in her teeth. The haze made breathing difficult and seeing a challenge.

The last frame was punctuated only by the grinding of Betty's teeth and the skip and crash of the bowling. She was ahead by eleven points when she finished. I needed a strike and two pins to win. As I toed the line, the gritching stepped up a couple decibels and became decidedly more manic. But I had been heckled by the best bar teams Knoxville had to offer. I slid it right into the pocket and got the strike. The boy set them up and I took out a bunch more – we didn't need to count how many – I had beat the old lady duckpin shark of Black Mountain.

"Well, you were good," she said. *Gritch gritch gritch.* "None of these ones can hardly ever beat me. I was married for thirty-five years."

"Thanks for the game, Miz B," I said, picking up my winnings from the bar. I now had eleven real dollars. That is, if you didn't count the two hundred or so twenty-first century dollars and the credit cards in my wallet – which you couldn't. Eleven dollars. By John's calculations, I could live well in this town for a week or two. Or stay and make my living as a duckpin hustler with Betty Bickerson. I suddenly needed comfort food.

"Count, would you make me up a cheeseburger and some fries and a Coke?"

"No fries," he said as he turned to the grill. "Chips. You want a Coke-coke or a Dr. Pepper-coke?"

"Coke-coke'll do, thank you."

Betty Bickerson sidled up to me at the counter. *Gritch gritch gritch.* Admiration, respect, something, shone in her watery eyes behind her dirty glasses. "You did good."

"Thank you, again, Miz B."

"You won my dollar."

"Yes. Yes, I did."

"Fair and square."

"Would you like a another hamburger, Miz B?"

"No cheese. It gums up my teeth."

"I see," I saw. "Uh, Count, would you make that all a double?"

"Already did," he said. The gang still hanging around the bowling alley nodded in approval. Many of them were studying the scoreboard, analyzing our game. The Count put the burgers on the counter, two waxed-paper bags of Tri-Sum potato chips, and two of those little bitty Cokes like they drank in *Grease*, about two good swallows in each bottle. Surprisingly though, the Coke tasted – well, good. Sweet, effervescent, somehow more solid than the last Coke I'd had back home. The burger, also small, was also delicious – juicy and crisp at the same time with pickles, mustard, tomato and lettuce – just the way I like it. The chips, however, were disappointingly stale.

As I pondered the small portions, and Betty ate half her burger and dribbled the other half on her blouse, another odd thing struck me. In my time (I could now think 'my time' without choking on it) it was common to see overweight people everywhere. Whole fat families, pods of chubby teens, marshmallow old couples tottering along. It was so common as to be unremarkable.

Here, I realized, I hadn't seen that many overweight people. Tiny, but he was big all over. I peered over the top of my baby Coke bottle; everyone in the bowling joint, everyone I could see through the windows on the street, was what you'd call thin to normal. I self-consciously sucked in my beer belly.

"Cute," Betty Bickerson said, chip crumbs falling with the word.

Not even wanting to imagine where this might be leading, I paid the Count the eighty cents for our two meals, fifty cents for the game, and left a generous thirty-cent tip. Less than two dollars, not bad for an evening's entertainment.

62 Jerald Pope

THE PIX

According to a neon-circled clock over the Count's grill, it was now a little after seven, still five hours until I was to meet Dale Ray at the jail. The sun was setting over the mountains down the valley, the air was starting to cool, it was a beautiful time of day. A few couples and families strolled the streets. Most seemed to be headed for the Pix, the movie theater across the street from Avena's. Tonight's offering was a double feature, *Red River*, which I remembered seeing (John Wayne does the cowboy Oedipus routine with Montgomery Clift) and *The Big Clock*, which I'd never heard of. The name was certainly synchronous with my situation, so I wandered over to look at the posters.

It starred Charles "Hunchback-of-Notre-Dame" Laughton and Ray "Lost-Weekend" Milland. The posters were so generic as to be useless. "The crime of your life" one of them stated, showing Ray looking worried, Charles looking ominous, and a tough dame looking confused. Smaller pictures, charmingly hand colored, had people pointing guns, leaning on desks, and lurking in dramatic shadows. Not a high-concept film.

A teenage girl came out from the little box office with a broom and began sweeping the already-clean sidewalk.

"So, how's 'The Big Clock?' I asked.

"Same goofy story," she said, as she swept. "Big-shot kills his girlfriend, frames Ray Milland, hires Ray to find the killer, which is him – the big-shot, not Ray. Oh, yeah, Ray was with the fellah's girlfriend before she died, but it was completely innocent, and he has a wife or a girlfriend or something. So they all meet behind the big clock for a shoot-out in New York City. I think."

"Okay. Well, I guess I don't need to see the movie now. Thanks for spoiling it for me."

"Gee, Mister, there's a lot more stuff I left out. The bad guy is Ray's boss, and he gets fired – I don't recall why…"

Just then the new police car cruised by. The girl stopped talking, stopped sweeping, stood up very straight and stared off to the West with an important look on her face, as if she were seeing the capital-F-future. The police car slowed down, and the driver – not Pug Morgan (this guy was handsome in a country-Russell Crowe sort of way) – lifted his hand from the window frame in a vague half-wave. She turned her head slightly and lifted her chin a half-inch in acknowledgment. He drove on, she relaxed and turned back to me. "What was I saying?"

"No, it's okay. So, what? You're into police cars?"

"Get into police cars? Why ever would I do that?" She started sweeping again in a distracted manner. "Oh, that? That's Arthur Joe, the town constable. He's over six feet tall. He doesn't know it, but he's gonna ask me to marry him one day."

"So you're dating a policeman?"

"No. I haven't actually talked to him yet. But I will, when the time is right. I know we were meant to be together."

"Uh huh. And how do you know that?"

She stopped sweeping and turned to me. "Because he's so tall and I'm so short. Because he's funny and strong and smart and has an important job. Because we both have blue eyes. Because his people have lived here forever. And because the heart wants what the heart wants. Gee, Mister, ain't you ever been in love?"

"Yes, yes, I have. I am. I'm getting married in two days, in fact."

"You are? That's nifty. Where's your bride?"

"Um. She's with her folks. I'm meeting them…soon."

"Congratulations, Mister. I can't wait til I get married."

"And how old are you?"

"Fifteen. Why?"

"Well, I hope you wait a few years."

"Why?"

'Well, you know. You might want to go to college or something."

"College!" She laughed as if I'd said she might want to be a fish. "I'm gonna be a *wife*. I probably won't even finish high school. I don't need any more book-learning. College!" She snorted in disbelief, shook her head, and with that, dismissed me.

The doors opened from the theater and the crowd from the six o'clock show began streaming out. Apparently they weren't sticking around for "The Big Clock." My slight interest in the movie evaporated and I joined the crowd, strolling down the street into the mellow summer night.

A big yellow moon was rising down at the end of State Street. And, yes, it did seem bigger and yellower than the moons I remembered seeing in the 21st century. Maybe it had something to do with pollution, or maybe with the fact that so many fewer lights lit up the night sky. Fewer, dimmer streetlights, fewer store lights, the cars' headlights themselves seemed dimmer. And no acres-big parking lots with their tall clusters of lights standing guard like towers in a prison yard, or creatures from *War of the Worlds*.

Couples, families, and a few solo strollers like me walked the street, chatting, laughing or in simple silence. I noticed the profound lack of peripheral noise; no ambient music, no swoosh and rumble from the non-existent interstate. The big, solid cars passed with a mechanical purr. They were steel and chrome and iron; I doubt if you could find two pounds of plastic in the whole of one of those marvelous machines.

Standing on that corner, in that night, I could understand Dale Ray's reluctance to return to our jittery, throwaway, over-informed, over-distracted present. The smell of some sweet, summery, grandmotherly flower wafted over me on a caressing breeze. I shuddered involuntarily in the warm air. The past was like the Land of the Lotus Eaters! I didn't belong here. I needed a drink. Maybe a cold watery beer would clear my head.

68 Jerald Pope

BACK TO DIXIE

I crossed the street to the unmarked door between the hardware store and the five and dime. Both stores were closed and dark, except for a single light bulb somewhere in the back of the dime store and a lit table lamp in the window of the hardware. The window was otherwise cluttered with rakes, shovels, a hand-pushed tiller, a gigantic and scary-looking chainsaw, cans of paint, a mop and a tackle box, closed. The street windows of the dime store were simply dark. The advantages of power window advertising obviously hadn't yet reached the merchants of Black Mountain.

The unmarked door sat in its gloomy niche, still unlocked. A couple gave me a suspicious glance, then ducked into the door. I followed them up the stairs, the man turning to shoot me another stare, in case I missed the first one. At the top, I met Dixie, coming out of the hallway to the right. "Hello Odell

Odell Lutz," she said, stopping to put on lipstick in the dim mirror. "You're still around."

"Yes I am, Dixie. I am in need of liquid refreshment. Seems this is the only watering hole in town."

"Oh, there's others. You just gotta know where. Come on in."

As we entered the coatroom, I could hear a fiddle playing. The untrusting couple opened the "secret" door and the music flooded out. A three-piece band was on the tiny stage at the far end of the room, banging away at a spritely tune. I didn't recognize it, but I recognized the style – mountain music, lots of notes. The dance floor was amazingly full. Although the room was dimly lit, I could see maybe twenty couples spinning around in a surprisingly lively fashion, given the heat they were generating. The usual cloud of cigarette smoke with hints of cigar hung in the air. I was getting used to the poison surprisingly fast. My grandparents had all smoked, before it killed three out of four of them, and when I was a kid, there wasn't much talk of it. My lungs were having their own trip down memory lane.

Tiny was still at the door. He was deep into the philosophy with an old man, but stood as the door opened. He saw me and his beetled brow furrowed even more. Then he saw Dixie and the furrow turned to simple resentment. "Fifty cents," he said.

"The judge is with me, Tiny," Dixie said reaching up to pat his cratered cheek as we passed. I resisted the impulse to do the same.

A crowd stood around the bar, men and women, drinking, laughing, smoking. A couple of waitresses were working the floor and Pete had a helper. Candles were now lit on the little tables – real candles in painted lamps. I couldn't tell through the haze if they continued the hula theme of the bar. Dixie went behind the bar to the cooler – she obviously had a proprietary interest in the joint- and pulled out a couple of cold bottles. I realized how thirsty I was, and also realized Dixie had changed her dress since the afternoon. "You changed your dress since this afternoon," I observed, as she led the way to a table.

"I do that a lot," she said. "It sorta goes with the job."

"Yeah? What job is that?"

"Oh, you know," she made a vague gesture that encompassed the room, the bar, the dancers, the ceiling fans.

"Fan repair?"

"More like 'fan-dancer,'" she turned and smiled lazily at me through the haze. Under the bright red lipstick that everyone wore (every female above fifteen, I mean) she had a nice smile. A very nice smile. Her protruding teeth were an unexpected aphrodisiac to me. I studied her as we wove through the dancers. She still had on the red earrings and necklace from earlier, but was now wearing a country cocktail dress. It was red, with big black polka dots, sleeveless, not cut too low in the front or back, with wide shoulder straps and flared at the waist, coming to about mid-calf.

We passed the mayor, dancing energetically with a matronly woman who might just be his wife. He had recovered nicely from his afternoon debauch. Dixie found an empty table, dumped the ashtray on the floor, put a couple of empty glasses on the tray of a passing waitress, and sat. "Now. What's your story, Odell Odell Lutz? You some salty dog, come in here, lookin' to get yourself in trouble?"

"No, no I am not, Dixie. I'm just killing time – so to speak. Waiting for an appointment. What's your story? Is this your fine establishment?"

"Huh! Wisht it was." She pulled a pack of cigarettes and a zippo lighter from somewhere, tapped out an unfiltered cigarette – I guessed filters hadn't been invented yet. Or cancer. She blew a luxurious cloud straight up into the general fog. "No, I'm just a workin' girl, trying to get by like everone else. Pete runs the place. Won't tell who owns it; it's quasi-illegal, as you might guess."

"'Quasi-,' eh?"

"Okay, all-illegal," she laughed. "But ever little tight-laced town in the world has a joint like this. Place for folks to blow off steam. Just, it's not usually smack dab in the middle of town like this one. But I bet you know all about joints and such."

"Well, sure. I guess. Where I come from, things are a little more, um, relaxed. It's not such a big deal."

"'Big deal!' I like that. 'Not such a big deal.' Where do you come from, Odell Odell? Up North somewhere, that's plain."

"Yeah, right. You got me. I'm from, well, New York City."

"No you are not. That is not a New York accent."

"What do you know about New York accents, small town girl like you?"

"I ain't a small town girl! I ain't from around here; I'm from Greenville, as a matter of fact."

"Oo, big city."

"I see what you're doin', changing the subject. Why'd you say you're from New York?"

"Okay, you got me. Baltimore."

"Uh uh."

"Richmond?"

"Better, but I don't think so."

"Knoxville?"

"I'd buy that. So why're you such a big liar, Odell Odell? What you got to hide?"

"How'd you get to be so good with accents?"

"Why do you always answer a question with a question?"

"Maybe I don't want to answer your question, ever think of that?"

She smiled (that smile again) and stubbed out her cigarette. "I thought so. You're on the run. That's why you're looking for Dale Ray."

"Maybe I am, but it's not something you want to be caught up in."

"You wanna get some air? This place is gettin' a little stuffy."

"Is it? I hadn't noticed."

"Come on, you." She led the way out behind the band to a landing on a flight of wooden stairs. They led down three stories to a dark alley. I could see people down there, mostly by the glow of their cigarettes. The landing was crowded too. Smoke flowed from the door like a foggy river.

"Hows about we go for a moonlight stroll?" she asked. Not waiting for a reply, she took my hand and threaded her way through the knots of people and down the stairs, which seemed to sway a bit from all the people standing on them. I guessed fire codes were a thing of the future too.

We made our way through the alley. This crowd seemed more relaxed than the one upstairs. Mostly people were just talking quietly, although at least two couples were involved in moderately heavy petting. This was the seedy underground of Black Mountain. Not that seedy, and not – apparently – that underground. Dixie was still holding my hand. I thought perhaps she needed steadying on the dirt and gravel terrain of the alley. I didn't mind.

We turned the corner and were on Broadway, down the hill from Avena's. His seemed to be the only open establishment at this time of night. The girl from the movie theater was outside Avena's, talking to her girlfriends. The new police car came around the corner. As if on cue, the girl turned from her friends, arched her back and stared off into the distance. This time she furrowed her brow, as if she saw something troubling on the horizon. Her friends apparently knew the drill; they smoothly closed the circle, leaving the girl out, and continued their conversation. The police car slowed and the driver nodded in the girl's direction. She turned slightly toward him and dipped her head toward her shoulder – an arcane acknowledgement that was perhaps less effective than some of the rest of her repertoire. It looked like she was trying to scratch her ear without using her hands. He watched her for a moment, then drove on.

"That girl," Dixie said. "She has set her cap for poor old Arthur Joe. He's got the hook in his jaw and don't even know it."

"How come you know it?"

"Everybody in town knows it. She tells everybody. She'll tell you, soon as she gets the chance."

"Already has."

"See."

We sat on an old wooden bench on the West side of the street. The moon was just clearing the buildings on the other side. It was the only light down at that end of the street. Dixie's hair seemed white, her red lips and fingernails were black in the moonlight. In her what-would-one-day-be-retro dress, she looked startlingly like one of the late-neo-Punk girls I dated in the 90's. I found my mind wandering to tattoos.

"You know, I have a kind of a weakness for outlaws," she said, looking at the moon.

"Yeah, I was sensing that."

"So if you was to tell me what kind of trouble you was in, maybe I'd be inclined to help you. In some way."

"I believe you would, Dixie." I paused, looking at her. She reached up and slowly rubbed the top of her nose, an oddly affecting gesture. She was, at that moment, the embodiment of the raw, innocent sensuality that I had been feeling since I dropped into this place – time. Her bare shoulder was touching my arm. I could smell the lingering hint of her perfume, mixed with sweat and tobacco. She was real and present in a way I hadn't seen, or felt, since adolescence first lifted me out of childhood. I was that close to a broken heart.

"But, you see," I finally said, "the first trouble is, I'm getting married in two days. More or less."

"More-or-less married, or more-or-less two days?"

"Two days. And the second one is, I've sort of lost my fiancée."

"Gee." She turned to look at me, her eyes lost in shadow. "How'd you do that? This is a little town."

"I know, I know. I made a wrong turn, not on purpose, and we got separated. I really am trying to get back to her."

"An you think ole Dale Ray's gonna help you? He's not a particularly trustworthy fellah, you know."

"Thanks, I'll keep that in mind."

"Where did you last leave this fiancée of yours? Maybe I can…"

"You're a doll, but I'm pretty sure I have to figure this out on my own."

"With Dale Ray."

"He's a, uh, interested party."

"Okay, but don't give him money."

"I'll remember that. Thanks."

We stood up. She was standing very close to me, her eyes still lost in the shadow of her bangs. "Well, Odell Odell, good luck."

"You know my name's not Odell Odell, right?"

"I know. But that's your outlaw name. I like outlaws. Do you mind if I...?" She reached her arms up around my neck, and paused, waiting for a sign from me. I didn't pause; I didn't think. I leaned into the shadow of her smile and kissed her red-black, bucktoothed mouth. It was a fairly chaste, 1940's movie-style kiss. And it was lovely.

"Not bad," she said, "for a Yankee." She turned and walked back up the alley. I watched her walk away until she stepped into the shadows and was gone.

I don't know how many other men have kissed some smoldering temptress who was not their wife two days before their wedding. Or not their mother. Not that Clarice is a smoldering temptress - or my mother either, for that matter. (Although, I did find some pictures and letters when I was helping Mom clear out the attic one time that made me wonder…. but that's another story.) From the movies and literature, you get the impression that a considerable number of grooms have faced that particular temptation. I felt guilty about it. I suppose I could say, technically, my fiancée wasn't born yet. But technically, neither was I. Bottom line – I did it. I'm glad I did it. And that is that.

A BLACK MOUNTAIN COLLEGE COMMENTARY

"That's a drag," a voice said from the moon-darkness of a doorway. A match flared, a cigarette glowed, then two. A tall man with dark curly hair and a big nose stepped out of the shadow. He was wearing one of those striped shirts that you would normally see on gondoliers in Venice, if you normally hung out in Venice – Italy, not California (gondoliers there had a whole other kind of shirt). He had on large blue jeans with rolled up cuffs and no shoes. His companion was a smallish young woman with long dark hair and sharply cut bangs under a dark-colored beret. She wore a peasant top and a black tights or leggings, also sans shoes.

They both stepped up close – too close, really – examining me as if I were an odd Appalachian marsupial.

"Ah," I said, "spied on by beatniks. Now there's an angle I wouldn't have expected."

"Beatniks!" the girl laughed in a German accent. "I love that! What does it mean?"

"You know," I started, then stopped. I vaguely knew that Kerouac and that crew were writing around about this time, but I was sure the Soviet satellite, Sputnik, and thus all things "nik," was still in the future. I left it at "you know."

"Sounds Russian," the man said. "You into that whole scene? Dostoyevsky, vodka, ballet?"

"Yeah. More Chekhov, though. Yearning, loss. So, what's the deal with you spying on me? Us."

The woman laughed. "He's got us, Merce."

Merce draped his arm casually over her shoulder. "The 'deal' is, sometimes we like to slip into town, catch the natives in their natural surroundings, without getting into a debate over aesthetics."

"I surmise from your outfits that you are not cowboys."

"Sort of an art student," said the woman.

"Teacher – kind of," said Merce.

"And you guys are out… romantically?" I said, loading my tone with as much approbation as I could. Teacher/student dating was frowned on in my era, although I had to admit, they made a cute couple.

"Just a field trip," Merce said. "We're very isolated up at the college."

"Culture clash?" I asked. I knew he was referring to Black Mountain College, somewhere east of town. Black Mountain in name only, it was a brief attempt to locate the avant-garde in the hills of Appalachia. An attempt that was met with general hilarity from the natives and focused insularity from what came to be regarded as a heavyweight field of artists in a variety of disciplines.

"Exactly. Well said."

"It's not mine," I admitted, although I couldn't say whose it was.

"Why'd you let her walk away, man?" the woman asked. "That was a beautiful moment."

"Yeah? If I'd known we had an audience...."

"Forget it, " Merce said. "That's what we do. We're artists. We watch; we observe, we try to understand; we make it into art."

"So," the woman repeated, "why did you let her go?"

I looked down the darkened street to the shadow where Dixie had disappeared. "Because I'm engaged?" I was surprised that it came out as a question.

They both shrugged as if they understood, if not completely agreed with, my answer. They were ahead of me.

"Tina," Merce said, "the ways of the heart are unknowable."

"Except," Tina replied, "the heart wants what the heart wants. I think, fellow, you will regret the road not taken for a long time."

"And only time will tell," I said. "To continue our collection of coffee cup aphorisms."

"Do you mean teacup aphorisms?" Tina asked. "You can't read anything on the bottom of a coffee cup."

The days of universal personal or humorous messages on our clothes and personal artifacts were still in the future. I simply shrugged in what I hoped was an aphoristic manner.

"Let's give him a dance," Merce said, dropping his cigarette and holding his hands out to Tina. "Our theme is Time and Loss."

She took one more heartfelt drag, let it out and threw her cigarette away. She lifted an eyebrow at me as if to say either "watch this" or "ow, I got a little smoke in my eye," and took his hands.

They stepped out into the moon-lit street, suddenly transformed into impossibly contained and elegant creatures. They pulled close together, looking into each other's eyes in such a way that I knew they must be lovers. They held for a moment, then pushed away and began moving in the street. The only sounds were the pad and slap of their feet, an occasional wisp of laughter from the alley, and their breath when they came close to me.

Their dance was rhythmical, but followed a time signature so complex, it seemed beyond rhythm. Their bodies orbited, touched, swayed like wheat or bedsprings, shuddered, clicked. They moved in and out of shadows, their own moon-shadows chasing them down the hill. It was a sad dance, speaking of desire, then yearning, then loss. Underlying it all, as with all decent art I suppose, was the sense of time, moving in different layers at different speeds; heartbeat, a life, the life of the world.

The dance was moving them away from me, down the hill, toward the tracks. A train called, not too far away, the haunting moan that only a steam engine can make. The dancers crossed the tracks, caught for a moment in the train's headlight. There was no cross-guard, no flashing lights or clanging bells. The train thundered through, not stopping. It was like a roaring mechanical curtain, signaling the end of their impromptu dance. The caboose passed and the train rumbled into the night. The dancers were nowhere to be seen. I closed my eyes for a moment, wanting to remember their gift, knowing – even as I tried – that it was already fading.

84 Jerald Pope

THE UN-JAILBREAK

I walked toward the tracks. Broadway ended there; I could see fields on the other side. Merce and Tina were gone, sunk back into the shadows. I turned on Sutton and walked past the station. In a solitary light, I could see a man in shirtsleeves and a hat, reading a newspaper. Bucolic "Nighthawks." Otherwise, this end of town was dead. I walked up the hill to the jail. Two white globes guarded either side of the door. I was a little early, but no one was around – no new police cars, no loiterers. I tried the door; it was unlocked, so I went in. The desk was vacant and the cell room was dark. I poked my head in. "Hello? Dale Ray? You there?"

"Yeah. There's a light switch on the left of the door."

I switched the light on and saw Dale Ray and Carl, sitting on their bunks in the cage, smoking. Dale Ray had his wonky glasses on. They both stood up as I entered the room. "What's the plan?" I asked.

"You're getting me outa here. Then we're gonna go – uh – see a man about a horse."

"Okay, but I don't have a lot of money."

"You don't need a lot of money."

"Well, how much is your bail?" My question caused Carl to snort a rheumy snort.

"You aren't *bailing* me out; you're *busting* me out."

"Whoa. A jailbreak? I don't think…"

"Shut up. It's not a jailbreak. More like a jail-lift. Come here."

I approached the cell cautiously. Dale Ray and Carl bent down and grabbed the bottom edge of the cage. "Grab ahold," Carl said.

I did as I was told, confused as to what we planned to accomplish. When we all had a good grip on the cage, Dale Ray said, "lift," and we lifted. The cage wasn't attached to the floor! It was heavy, but three men could pick up the side. When it was about two feet off the ground, Dale Ray slid one of the stools under the edge. We set the edge down on the stool, and he slid out, underneath the cell.

"You need anything, Carl?'

"I'm fixed up, Dale Ray. Maybe a bottle of beer. Pack of cigareets, if you think about it."

"You got it. Come on – what's your name?"

"Odell Lutz."

"You any relation to the Lutzes, live up in Lytle Cove?" Carl asked.

"I'm pretty sure I'm not. But you never know. Aren't you going to get in trouble, sneaking out like this?"

"Nah. Nobody'll be in 'til the morning," Dale Ray said. "We do it all the time. Let's go, Liddell. I don't want to miss the show."

"Show?"

"You'll see. You wanna go home? Let's get going."

Dale Ray had shed his shaky wino image and was on a mission. I liked that. We walked out of the police station and around the corner to a little alley between the fire station and a one-story river stone building. In the middle of the building was a large window. The room was dimly lit by a glass-shaded lamp. A long box leaned toward the window. I glanced inside, then stopped. "Is that what I think it is?"

"If you think it's Ida Burnett, yes, it is."

"An open coffin in a window?"

"It's for drive-through viewing. Makes it real convenient for folks – old-timers who can't walk so good: people in a hurry for some reason. Pretty clever, I thought."

"No, it's creepy."

"Careful, buddy. It was my idea. I passed it on to Mr. Vandiver. He liked it."

"Aren't you afraid you're going to screw up the time-matter continuum, introducing ideas from the future?"

"Yeah, I try to be careful. I don't know what a paradox might do, but I don't want to risk it."

"But you did this time."

"I was drunk."

"Oh, well, okay then."

A WALK ACROSS TOWN

We walked east on State Street, past the Pix, past what Dale Ray told me was the famous Apron Lady's shop. State Street was also the main highway through town. It was lined with service stations. Apparently the climb up the mountain took its toll on the various pre-war jalopies that made it. As we walked, Dale Ray told me about his life before, as an engineer designing parts for oil field equipment, or something (I didn't really pay that much attention), and his life now as a con-man and general town drunk (I paid close attention, not wanting this to become *my* life).

We were lit only by the moon, now almost overhead, and the occasional passing car or truck. At the edge of town we turned onto Flat Creek Road. The high school was on the right, closed for the summer and looking forlorn and abandoned. In the distance a car was coming down the street toward us. As it got closer, we stepped out of the road – there were no sidewalks at this end of town.

The car lights resolved themselves into the town police car. As it drove closer, I looked around. Sure enough, the ticket girl was standing in the moonlight in the high school parking lot as if she'd just gotten out of class- two months, a day and six hours ago. She shot a glance at the car, ran her hand through her hair, put her shoulders back, and struck her historically distracted pose. This time, the police car stopped and the driver leaned out the window to talk to her. Dale Ray and I stood, watching the town's most famous mating dance. After a brief conversation, the girl shook her head, but in a coquettish fashion. The cop got out of the car, offered her his arm, and walked her around to the passenger side. He opened the door for her, she sighed theatrically, and got in to the car.

"The eagle has landed," Dale Ray said. "That girl has been…"

"I know all about it, Dale. What? You think I just got off the bus?"

"Well, let's hope it works out," he said, as the car drove away and we continued our walk. "Arthur Joe is as dense as a box of rocks where it comes to romance."

"Right. You know him from the jail."

"He's sorta what you might call my second boss. Tells a good story, though. Did you know there's bear hunting clubs? They own land, hunt bears with dogs, eat the meat, everything."

"I did not know that."

"Speaking of romance, one time Arthur Joe and a couple of his buddies picked up two girls hitchhiking here in town. This was back when he was a kid. Said they needed a ride to Old Fort. Well, the boys figured they could take them to Ridgecrest, that's just up the hill a ways."

"Uh huh."

"So they get to Ridgecrest, and they're getting along pretty good, so the boys say they'll take them down the mountain to Old Fort. Well they just about get to Old Fort, and the girls say, 'Actually, we're going to Marion,' which is another ten, twelve miles further on. This is a little weird, but these country boys are just so excited to be riding around with some strange women – I mean, strangers to them – that they say, 'Okay, we'll take you on to Marion.'

"So they get to Marion, and, sure enough, the girls say, 'Really, we live in Spruce Pine,' which is *way* back up in the mountains, near the Parkway. But the boys are committed this far, and – I don't know- maybe there's a hint of romance in the air, so they agree to take 'em on up to Spruce Pine.

"Well, they get up there, and they are having a good time, and, don't you know it, the girls say, 'You know what? We actually live in Bakersville. Could you just take us on home?' So these goofy boys get some gas and drive on to Bakersville, then outside it to a little country lane, up a mountain, across a stream, to this house. As soon as the pull up in the yard, this old lady comes out the screen door and the girls say, 'Bye' and scoot inside.

"Now this old lady is looking hard at these boys, so Arthur Joe, being a young gentleman at heart, gets out to go introduce himself, assure her nothing bad was going on. Well, he gets up and sees this woman and about turns white as a sheet. Seems like she is the spitting image of his grandma, who he had helped bury not a month earlier. He tells her this and apologizes for acting so squirrely, and she says, 'Why, you're Essie's boy! I'm your grandma's sister!' and she pinches his cheek. Seems he'd run all over creation, trying to put the make on his very own cousin."

I pondered this story for a bit as we trudged on up the road. "Kind of a Southern thing, isn't it."

"Yep. I reckon."

"Dale Ray, where'd you come from? Before you ended up here?"

"Chapel Hill. I was an economics professor. Tenure track, if you can believe it."

"I thought you were a mechanical engineer."

"Oh, that too."

"And this is better than that? Really?"

"Oh, yes. Really. Did I tell you about my girlfriend?"

"Here or there?"

"Definitely here. My wife would never go along with me having a girlfriend back in the future."

Aha. Apparently my twisted sophistry about the Dixie kiss was a common ploy of the time travelling crowd. Damn. I filed that one away for future contemplation. "So. Where are we headed, Dale?"

"It's Dale Ray. Roseland Gardens. It's a juke joint up the road a ways. Place for black folk to get together, relax, when they're not serving the Man."

"What do you mean? What man?"

"You know, the Man."

"Oh, him. Right."

"A lot of the white people who summer up here bring their maids, chauffeurs, nannies, whatever. Their gardeners, for all I know. When they get a night off, there's really no place to go but Roseland Gardens. This is a pretty relaxed little town in some ways, but it's still the South, and Martin Luther King is still just a kid."

"Are they going to take kindly to a couple of white men dropping in?" I was thinking about my earlier encounter.

"Oh, Horace is pretty relaxed about that. As long as you don't start trouble."

"Is that who we're going to see? Horace?"

"No… you'll see. We're almost there."

94 Jerald Pope

ROSELAND GARDENS

We'd been walking along Flat Creek Road for about a mile. I could hear the creek running off to the left. Darkened farmhouses, fields and barns lined the road, with occasional clusters of newer houses. As we approached what turned out to be a crossroad, the road seemed to wake up. A little store was open on the corner with some people standing around. Up the hill to the right, a house party was in full swing – lights blazing, music blaring from a record player, people coming and going.

Ahead of us, up the creek , a house and a low barn-sided structure snuggled up against a hill, connected with strings of colored lights. Between them and up and down the street, various cars were parked. People were sitting on the cars, walking around, chatting. I could hear music coming from the barn, smell barbecue, see men in suits and hats, women in party dresses coming and going. It was as if all the random, late night activity in town had been distilled, concentrated, and splashed with cologne. Dale Ray swept his hand like a magician. "Roseland Gardens," he said. "You hungry?"

I was. We went around behind the barn where a low, attached shed sweated smoke, grease and goodness. Inside was a rough counter behind which several women were serving up sandwiches, barbecue plates, and bottles of beer and soda. A line of people waited with money in their hands. They all looked hot; the men had their jackets off and handkerchiefs out, the women were dabbing at their faces and chests with their own more delicate handkerchiefs. Through the wall of the kitchen, I could hear the source of their exertion – a band was rocking and a woman was shouting the blues. "For a dry town, there sure is a lot of alcohol flowing."

"This way both the Baptists *and* the Presbyterians are happy," Dale Ray said. "I'll have a plate and a beer. You pay."

I ordered and we received our food on china plates, with a fork wrapped in a very old and threadbare cloth napkin. The cashier, who was sitting in a kitchen chair at the end of the line, making change out of a cigar box, didn't look up as I paid. "Two plates, two beers, one dollar," she said. I took the plates, Dale Ray grabbed the beers and we made our way outside to a random collection of tables and chairs where people were eating. Picnic tables, kitchen tables, dining room sets were scattered about – all weathered and all occupied.

"Mind if we join you?" Dale Ray said to a couple sitting at a four top. He was in suspenders and a straw hat; she had on a low-cut green dress and yellow earrings.

"We was actually saving them for our friends," the man said.

"Okay," Dale Ray said, looking around. "We can sit on the wall." He nodded me toward a low stone wall that was caught in a losing struggle with the hill.

"Dale Ray?" the man looked up from under the brim of his hat. "Is that you? Man, I thought you were still in the hoosegow."

"Hey, Wool. Naw, I'm taking the night off. Hey, Primadonna, how's it going?"

"It's goin' good, Dale Ray," the woman said, smiling. "Glad to see you out."

"Just for the evening. It was such a pretty summer night, I couldn't let it slide by."

"I know what you mean, man," Wool said. "Pull on up."

"This is my friend, Otis. Otis, Wool and his lady, Primadonna."

"Dale Ray…" Primadonna giggled.

"Actually, it's 'Odell'," I said, shaking Wool's hand.

"Uh huh," Wool said. "You and Dale Ray go way back, right?"

"All the way back to three o'clock," I said.

"Sounds about right. Sit down, don't let your pig get cold."

We sat down and dug in. It was the typical Southern trinity; pulled pork, greens, and butter beans. The meat was okay, very smoky but a bit dry, and the beans were good, but the collards were like heaven. Buttery soft, cooked in lard (of course) with a hint of vinegar and an spice I couldn't identify that knocked them out of the park. "Wow," I said.

"I know," said Dale Ray. "Put some of this sauce on your meat."

A half-full mason jar on the table held a thick red sauce. I lathered it on pretty good. It woke the meat up, made it tangy and complex. "Now this is barbecue," I muttered through a full mouth.

"Otis's not from around here," Dale Ray laughed. "He's from… Charlotte?"

"Knoxville. Is there any more of that sauce?"

"They don't get decent barbecue over there."

Wool leaned back and borrowed the jar from another table. "I was in Knoxville once," he said. "During the War. Big."

"Pretty big," I said. "But I think it's going to get bigger."

Dale Ray shot me a glance and was about to say something, when a commotion began at the table next to ours. Two women were standing, leaning across the table, yelling in each other's faces. The men with them stood up and backed away from the table, awkward smirks on their faces. One of the women reached out and slapped the other. Now everyone was standing, to get a better view or get out of the way. I grabbed my plate – I wasn't finished – and Dale Ray grabbed both our beers. The slapped woman reached over and grabbed a double handful of hair, pulling her opponent down with the table, chairs, and whatever plates, bottles, and food had been on the table.

Suddenly, a completely round man in a cowboy hat pushed through the circle that was forming, grabbed the two women by their arms and jerked them to their feet. "Horace," Dale Ray said.

"I enjoy a good catfight as much as the next man," Horace said in a surprisingly deep bass voice. "But I won't tolerate you all breakin' up my furniture."

This got an appreciative laugh from the crowd and the fight seemed to drain out of the women. "Now you girls want to take it out to the street, or are you done?" Horace asked. They hung their heads, glaring a little at each other silently. He shook their arms. "I asked you a question. What's it gonna be? Street or done?"

"Done," they said in unison.

"All right. Now pick up this mess and be on about your business. The rest of you folks go on, too. Little girl's 'bout to sing again inside. You know you don't want to miss that."

The women began picking up the table and their partners pitched in to help them. Horace, who really was as round as he was tall, hitched up his belt and looked around. I saw he wore two guns on his belt – two big, forty-five, cowboy-looking guns. His eye caught the two white men standing out in the crowd. He did a little double take, then started over toward us. "Dale Ray. I thought you were in the pokey. What're you doin' up this way?"

"Taking a vacation from my vacation, Horace. I want you to meet my friend, Otis from Nashville. Otis, this is Horace Rutherford, the black sheriff of Black Mountain."

"Pleased to meet you, Mister Rutherford," I said, shaking his hand.

"Otis Nashville, eh? Not from around here?"

"It's Odell, and, no, not exactly."

"Well, any friend of Dale Ray's is a man I want to keep an eye on. So make yourself at home, but keep your nose clean, if you know what I mean."

"Yes, sir, I do," I said, though I didn't.

"We were actually hoping to run into Atticus," Dale Ray said.

"He been around tonight?"

"No, but I expect he will be. It's early yet."

"The joint is jumpin' tonight."

"Yeah, it's Juneteenth, you know. Liberation Day."

Just then, a skinny little girl about six years old in pigtails and a pink nightgown came running up. "Grandpa! What happened? Was it a fight? Who was it? What did I miss?"

Horace rolled his eyes at us and bent down to the girl. His bending down being more of a rolling-down motion. "Miss Katherine. What have I told you about comin' out here at night? What?"

"I'm not s'posed to," Miss Katherine pouted.

"That's right. So what are you doin' here in the middle of what you're not supposed to?"

"Well, I was just watchin' from my window, and I heard a terrible commotion, and I… I thought you might need some help, so I came."

"That don't cut it, girl. You get back in that house and you stay there. I catch you out here again, it'll mean your hide. You understand me?"

"Grandpa?"

"Yes, sugar?"

"Who's that man?" She pointed at me.

"Not none of your business, and you're just stallin'. Now git." He gave her a swat and she ran off through the crowd. "That girl has no business being out here this time of night," he said, looking fondly after her. "I don't expect Atticus for a while. You boys might as well come in, hear this little girl from down the mountain somewhere. Tryon? She's good."

We filed into the hall. At the door, a bouncer was taking money and checking for stamped hands. "How much?" I asked. The bouncer looked at Horace, but he kept his face unreadable. No complimentary tickets here.

"Fifteen cents, each," the bouncer said. I handed over a quarter and a nickel. Dale Ray patted my shoulder in reward. Inside it was crowded, smoky, and hot. The room smelled of sweat, cologne, and cigarettes. The place was lit with red, blue, and yellow light bulbs along the wall, with four white bulbs over the stage. A tiny bandstand at the far end held an upright piano. A doghouse bass and a three-drum trap set were crowded on the stage behind a single microphone. A guitar leaned against the piano and a shiny trumpet lay on top. The band was returning from their break. A large fan was built into the wall behind the band, turning slowly, pushing fresh air into the room. Unfortunately, the air only made it about two feet past the bandstand before it was overwhelmed.

Horace Rutherford squeezed his way to in front of the bandstand- there would have been no room for him on it, even without the band. Someone handed him down the microphone. "All right, everybody," he rumbled into the mike. "Let's welcome her back. Out for good behavior from the Allen School for Girls, Eunice Wayman!"

A slight, reserved-looking young woman walked up on the stage and sat down at the piano. She wore a red, short-sleeved blouse over a navy knee-length pleated skirt. She had a thin white scarf holding her hair up off her neck. It looked very patriotic. She started playing something rather classical. The band waited as did the crowd. After some fancy arpeggios, she slid into a bluesy riff that got a shout from the crowd. The band followed after her – they were tight and loud, though un-amplified. The girl, Eunice, began to sing the old Bessie Smith number, "Black Mountain Blues":

> *Out in Black Mountain a child will smack your face*
> *I'm saying out on Black Mountain a child will smack your face*
> *The babies cry for liquor, and all the chickadees sing bass*
>
> *Well, out in Black Mountain you can't keep a good man in jail*
> *Yeah, out in Black Mountain you can't keep a good man in jail*
> *'Cause if the jury convicts him, the judge just go his bail*

Her voice sounded familiar. Dale Ray and I stood shoved against the wall with the other wallflowers as couples danced, slow and close. This was my second dose of heat, sweat, smoke, perfume, and music in one night. I felt like I was really starting to get in touch with my animal nature. Dixie's kiss, which I had put out of my mind, kept coming back to haunt me in disturbing ways.

They finished "Black Mountain Blues" to polite, distracted applause. After a couple more songs, a wave of dancers left the floor, headed outside for fresh air (at least) and another wave took their place. The band started into the Gershwin tune, "I Loves You, Porgy." I knew immediately why the singer sounded familiar.

"My god!" I said. "That's Nina Simone! Only she's seventeen!"

"Who?" Dale Ray asked, leaning in to hear me over the music.

"Nina Simone. Don't you remember? Oh man, she was a big jazzy, bluesy, pop star from the Fifties- or Sixties. Exiled to France for being against the Vietnam War, or something."

"What war you talking about?" A short man in a moss-colored suit who was standing in front of me turned around, a quizzical look on his face.

"East China," Dale Ray said, grabbing my arm. "McHale's Navy. Behind-the-lines stuff." He dragged me toward the door.

"Hey! I want to hear this! This is historic!"

"Shut up, you idiot. Come outside."

We walked away from the building toward the street. When we were clear of other people, Dale Ray turned to me. "Listen. You may be trying to get out of here, back to whatever little futuristic deal you got going, but this is my life. And you are not gonna screw it up."

"Relax, Dale Ray. I didn't say anything."

"Vietnam? Nina Simoleon? Those things don't exist yet."

"Nina *Simone*; she's a very important jazz lady. I forgot she was from North Carolina."

"She's nobody. She's a kid. Eustace Somebody from Wherever. You get people asking questions, wondering about you and the next thing you know, you're headed for the loony bin. And you'd better believe it will happen."

"You mean...?"

"There's been people. A woman that I actually knew. I've heard of others. Lobotomies are very popular right now, you know."

"Ulp."

"That's right, ulp. And, understand me, I will cut you loose, if it comes to that. These are paranoid times; the big Commie Scare is coming."

"So it's not all Mayberry and Aunt Bee's apple pie."

"You know it's not. No place – no time – is. But I've found my place here. And you're not going to ruin it for me."

"Not going to ruin it for any of us," a voice from behind us said. Dale Ray and I spun around like doo-wop choreography. Standing there was the man I'd passed on the stairs, going up to the speakeasy. He held out his hand. "Atticus Crow, local attorney and good ole boy."

"Pleased to meet you, Mister Rutherford

"Odell Lutz." I shook his hand.

"A pleasure, Mr. Lutz. Dale Ray. How goes it?"

"So far, so good, Atticus. You moving a little product tonight?"

"Never can tell, Dale Ray," Atticus said, putting his finger beside his nose. "Never can tell. So, Odell. From what I overheard, Dale Ray was berating you for a little indiscretion. Am I correct?"

"Do you know who that singer is? That's…"

"Eunice Wayman. I know. Quite a nice voice. I actually arranged this engagement for her. I heard her play a recital in Asheville."

"Really? Cool. But, you know, she's going to be…"

"Going back to school soon. That's all we know, Odell. Do you understand? I appreciate that you're a jazz aficionado, but what Dale Ray was telling you is ever so true. There are those of us who have made a nice place here. We wouldn't want to disturb that."

"Okay. I get that. I don't want to mess you guys up. I do want to get back to… to my own, um, hometown."

"Good. Well said. Dale Ray, would you like to help the sheriff load my car? There's five dollars in it. Odell and I are going to take a walk."

"I got it covered," Dale Ray said, and headed off toward the house.

A WALK ALONG THE CREEK

Atticus took out a cigar, did not offer me one, rolled it in his mouth and lit it. We walked away from Roseland Gardens, up the road. "So. You've been doing a little travelling."

Suddenly, it struck me. "You're the guy we're supposed to meet! You're the guy that can get me out of here!"

"Possibly. There are no guarantees." His eyes glittered under the brim of his hat. His ice cream suit seemed to glow in the moonlight. "Do you know about string theory, Odell?"

"I've heard about it. New math, new physics, something like that. I used to read a lot of science fiction."

"Quantum physics."

"Right!"

"Good. In a nutshell, Time and Matter are not linear. Well, they are, but… in a nutshell, they're not. Let's say Time is like a plate of spaghetti; wherever a piece of spaghetti touches another piece, or bends around and touches itself, that's a potential nexus or transfer point. Get it?"

"Uh, sure. Go on."

"You said you were a science fiction fan; it's like a wormhole, a shortcut between places, so you don't have to travel along the whole spaghetti. But it's also a place where different times bump into each other."

"So it's more Star Trek: Deep Space Nine than regular Star Trek."

"You're a regular Einstein. In the physical world, these nexuses manifest where fissures in the earth meet, around unusual rock formations, big crystal formations, waterfalls, volcanoes, that sort of stuff. Humans have always been drawn to these power places, often without understanding why. They build monuments, temples, and most often, cities on them."

"Yeah, I read where Asheville was built on a giant crystal or something."

"Or something. Not just Asheville, most large cities in America are. The exceptions are Detroit, Chicago, Atlanta, Los Angeles, and, of course, Las Vegas. You just have to look at the histories of those places to see this is true."

"What about Knoxville?"

"Stay focused, Mr. Lutz. Black Mountain has its own share of nexuses; that's probably what draws all the religious retreat centers around here. We don't know how the connection between the physical and the temporal works, but there can be keys that open the doors between the spaghettis."

"Or the parts of the *same spaghetti*."

"Yes, very good."

"I'm with you. How do you identify these keys? Are they always the same or different?"

"Excellent questions. Sometimes through trial and error, sometimes there's history, legends, sometimes you can just figure it out, logically."

"So the Elvis tooth…"

"Exactly. It's a key. There may be more, but we know this one. And the lock – the place where the key works… "

"Is the Time Shop."

"Right."

We were standing on a little bridge over Flat Creek. The moon was doing a Cubist dance on the water. Trees hung their shadows toward the stream. It was a perfect summer night. I took out my phone to check the time; it was after four.

"Hm. I haven't seen one of those in a while," Atticus said, taking the phone from my hand. His fingers flew over the screen, bringing up programs I never knew existed. Screens and text were flying. "The old Tangxia factory model," he said. "I'd forgotten about these. Guangdong province. They had a few bugs and a secret relayer the Chinese built in that Apple didn't know about. I disabled it and cleaned out some programming you don't need. That'll be faster for you – more efficient."

He handed the phone back to me. I checked the time. It was still a little after four. "So, Atticus. What year are you from?"

"Twenty sixty-five. Very depressing time. I was quite happy to leave it and come here."

"What's depressing about it? Is there still an America?"

"Of course. But the world is even more over-populated than it was in your day. Have you noticed how people just stopped talking about population control? It's as if we collectively decided the topic was moot; as if we all agreed we were going to breed and breed until there was no room left to stand."

"No, I actually hadn't noticed that, what with all the other problems we have. Had. Will have."

"Yes. So we pushed all the other species off into extinction, except the ones we want for food. That coupled with the advances in science that allow more and more people to live to a hundred and fifty, even more. It was just depressing."

"Gosh. I could conceivably live to the Sixties."

"It's conceivable. But do the Earth a favor. Don't conceive."

"Well, you get me back, and I'll do my best."

"I hope you will." He threw his cigar butt into the stream.

"Get back, or do my best?"

"Both, Odell. Both."

"So how do I get back? First, how do I get to 1976?"

"Why would you want to go there?"

"To meet Elvis; get the tooth."

"Well, you'd be a year late. Elvis will be dead by then."

"But Dale Ray said…"

"Dale Ray always gets it wrong. I sometimes wonder if he does it on purpose." We started walking back to Roseland Gardens. "You want to be here on July twenty-third, 1975, Odell. Not a day later."

"And how – exactly – do I do that? I mean, what if I land in '74? Do I have to wait around for a year? Or what if I land in some other year? Or March, for god's sake."

"It appears that the places where the, um, spaghetti touches are stable. You should arrive very close to the appropriate time. I believe it relates to the key. It apparently acts like a beacon."

"That's a relief. I guess. Say, how do I get from here-now to '75?"

"The same way. There's a key."

112 Jerald Pope

"Do you have it?"

"No, I don't. But I believe it's here at Roseland Gardens. There's a logical connection between Blues music and Elvis Presley. We just have to find the right key."

"You mean there's a wrong key?"

"Oh, lots. You could end up meeting Davey Crockett, for example."

"In Black Mountain? He lived here?"

"Passed through. It wasn't Black Mountain then, though. This would have been the very early nineteenth century."

"Okay. I *really* don't want to go there."

"I think we can, with some assurance, see that you meet your appointment with the King. Oh, I should tell you; it's quite possible you won't be the only one vying for the tooth."

DESPERADOS

We sauntered back up to Roseland where Dale Ray and a couple of other men were standing around Atticus Crow's car, smoking. It was a new-looking, gigantic blue sedan with wooden sides and white walls that were at least six inches wide. It was the biggest, boxiest car I'd ever seen; it looked like the Hummer's grandpa.

"What kind of car…?" I started to ask.

"Chrysler Imperial," Atticus and the three other men chorused, simultaneously.

"Nineteen forty-eight," said Atticus, with pride. "There's never been such a luxurious piece of highway machinery."

The grill was a vast expanse of chrome that went on forever, seeming to draw its inspiration from the Imperial Palace in

China (thus, perhaps, the name). The hood and front fenders took up half the length of the car; I couldn't imagine what sort of beast the engine was. The trunk looked small by comparison, yet I was pretty sure you could put an entire Volkswagen in there – as soon as they were imported.

The trunk was open and Atticus leaned in to inspect the contents – about ten cases of mason jars filled with clear liquid. Horace Rutherford waddled up, smoking a cigar.

"It's all there, counselor."

"I know it is, Horace. But you know I have to count it anyway."

"I'm a little confused here," I said, scratching my head. "Isn't it risky for a lawyer to be running moonshine? What if the cops caught you?"

Just then a car pulled slowly into the parking lot, its wheels crunching the gravel. The headlights swept across us, then a light mounted by the driver's side turned on, catching us all in its brightness. Another light – a flashing red light – spun briefly on the roof of the car, then turned off.

"Like this," I said, as we all froze.

The policeman turned off the car, turned off the lights and stepped out. As my eyes grew re-accustomed to the dark, I saw that it was the new Mercury police cruiser.

"Dammit, Pug," Dale Ray said. "Not funny."

Horace took his cigar out of his mouth and spat a piece of tobacco onto the ground. "For a minute there," he said, "I thought you were that new deputy sheriff comin' around to make trouble."

Pug Morgan walked up, with a smirk on his face, obviously proud of his little cop joke. "Boys. Everything all right here?"

Atticus shook his hand. "Pug. I'm just getting ready to go down to Raleigh. It's the legislature's summer retreat. I'm providing the refreshment."

"Good," Pug said, taking a jar out of the Chrysler. "Bring 'em something decent. They can't make no good law drinking that flatland swamp water."

He opened the jar and sniffed. "This ain't Madison County shine is it?"

"No sir," said one of the loaders. "Made right up the mountain here in Montreat."

"Good. Holy water, it's the best." He lifted the jar and toasted us, then took a sip. "Not bad. That's Burnett recipe, if I'm not mistaken."

"You have an educated palate, Pug," Atticus said. "Pass that around. I believe we've all earned a little refreshment."

Pug handed the jar to Horace, who took a sip and passed it on. Each man was conservative in his tasting, muttering appreciative sounds. Only Dale Ray took a long pull on the jar. I was the last in line. I had tasted moonshine back in Knoxville, where it was more a novelty than a serious drinking liquor. The Burnett recipe was clean and burning with hints of smoke, laurel, and hops. Still not something I would sit down to an evening of recreational drinking with.

As I handed the jar back to the police chief, he eyed me quizzically. "And who might you be?"

"He *might* be Davy Crockett, Pug," Dale Ray said. "But he is my old friend, Beau Dean Butz, just up from Charlotte."

I stuck out my hand. "Odell Lutz, just over from Knoxville."

Pug gripped my hand in a serious, police-style grip. "Odell. What brings you to Black Mountain? How are you messed up with this bunch of snake-handlers?"

"Well," I started.

"Odell's going to accompany me down the mountain," Atticus put in, quickly. "He's my protection for the trip. I don't like to go naked unto the wilderness when I'm carrying this much valuable tax-free merchandise."

"That right? What's your weapon of choice, Odell?"

"Well, you know," I began.

"I feel fairly certain Odell's skill with this will see me through." Atticus reached into the trunk and pulled out a sawed off shotgun with a bore enormous enough to satisfy Yosemite Sam. He handed it to me.

"Yep," Dale Ray said. "'Ten-gauge Odell' we used to call him."

I carefully aimed the gun at the ground and broke it open to see if it was loaded. It was. "Yep," I said.

Just at that moment, five young men approached us. They all wore hats and in the shadows you could see they had scarves over their faces. They all had their hands ostentatiously in their pockets. They walked right up to us in an obviously planned and rehearsed manner. The apparent leader coughed and they all drew pistols from their pockets. They were small caliber, nickel-plated guns that looked almost cute to my jaded eye, soaked as it was in 21st century high-caliber, extra-magazine mayhem.

"Put em up, fellahs," the lead robber said. "We just want the money."

Pug Morgan, his police badge shining in the moonlight, put his hand on the Colt thirty-eight he was wearing; Horace Rutherford reached up to his armpits and put both hands on his two forty-fives; I closed the shotgun with a satisfyingly loud click; Dale Ray and the two other loaders stepped up behind us. We made a formidable phalanx for any parking lot hijacking.

"There isn't any money, yet," Atticus said. "It's the beginning of the run. You're supposed to rob us *after* the run."

A murmur rose from the gang. The leader raised his gun and pointed it at Atticus' face. "We knew that. I meant to say we're gonna take the booze. And that car."

"No, you're not," Atticus said.

"Whadda you mean? Yes, we are."

"Man said no," said Pug, drawing his pistol.

"We'll shoot you. We don't even care," one of the other men said in a trembly voice that belied what he was saying. He raised his gun. The other three followed suit.

Horace drew his pistols. I was impressed with how smoothly he manipulated the large, awkward guns. I raised the barrel of the shotgun, but resolved that – whatever happened – I wasn't pulling the trigger.

"Before we jump into this," Dale Ray said, stepping forward, "let's do a little math. You boys seem pretty new to this game. You got your five little pea-shooters lined up against three big caliber revolvers, a very nasty sawed-off shotgun, and this tommy-gun that Rufus has back there, all in the hands of experienced veterans who have actually killed their fellow man. And at least one of them, I know for a fact, enjoyed doing it. Seems to me, it don't add up in your favor." He let that sink in for a moment, then said, "'Course, the choice is yours."

There came a pregnant pause.

I could almost hear the desperados' eyeballs clicking back and forth in the shadows of their hats, looking for someone to tell them what to do.

Horace harumphed dismissively. "Y'all either start slingin' lead or git," he said.

They made their choice. The robber with the trembly voice backed quickly into the shadows. The other four followed, holding their guns toward us and glancing behind them to make sure they didn't fall over something.

"You all are… just… darn lucky!" a voice called out from the dark, followed by the sound of running feet.

Our gang let out our collective breath. Pug, who was still holding the Mason jar, passed it around again.

"'Slinging lead'?" Atticus asked, taking a large swallow and passing the jar to Horace.

"I always wanted to say that," Horace said smiling and wiping the sweat from his face.

"The not-ready-for-prime-time criminals," I toasted the absent thieves, laughing with the relief of not having to fire a sawed-off shotgun for the first time in my life.

Atticus and Dale Ray shot me warning looks. "Prime time," said one of the loaders. "That's good. What does it mean?"

"Ah, 'big-time' is what I meant. 'Not ready-for-big-time criminals.' I just, um, made a stupid rhyme because I was nervous. 'Big-time.'"

"Nah. It doesn't work as good. I like 'prime-time.' I'm gonna remember that one."

"Well, we should really be going," Atticus muttered, darkly. "Dawn'll be here soon enough."

"Yeah," Dale Ray said. "I need to be getting back down to the jail. Wouldn't want to cause any up-right police chief any extra trouble."

"You need a ride, Dale Ray?" Pug asked.

"No, I'm all right. I've got a few things I want to finish up here."

"Okay, then. You boys be careful," Pug said, as he walked back to his car. "Now, those were some pathetic criminals. Not ready for prime-time, not ready at all."

I didn't need to look to feel the eyes burning holes in the back of my head. Atticus counted out a stack of bills into Horace's hand, then gave Dale Ray and the other two helpers each a bill.

"Pleasure doing business with you, counselor," Horace said. He tipped his cowboy hat to Dale Ray and me and wandered back toward his establishment.

"We have got to get this bozo out of here," Dale Ray said to Atticus. (I was pretty sure I knew which bozo he was referring to.) "He's going to ruin it for everybody."

"Sorry," I said. "It's trickier than it looks, keeping up with your anachronisms."

THE MONTREAT GATE

Atticus took the shotgun from my hands and put it in the trunk of the Chrysler with the moonshine, then closed it gently. "If the worst thing he does is introduce 'prime-time' into the lexicon, we're fine. Now let's see if we can find that key."

"What are we looking for?" I asked.

"Nothing specific," Atticus said, locking the Chrysler. "It'll be small, able to fit in your pocket. It'll have a certain numinesence."

"Numi-what?" I said.

"Atticus likes to throw around those three-dollar words. He's a student of Carl Jung," Dale Ray explained. "Something that seems unusual or out of place, or just a thing that catches your eye."

A popsicle stick lying on the ground, glowing in the moonlight caught my eye. "Like this?" I said holding it up.

"Probably more specific than that," Atticus said. "Although you have the right idea. It could be anything. Put that in your pocket."

We fanned out across the parking lot, which was well-seeded with bottle caps and cigarette butts. None of them seemed numinescent. The lot filled up with people as Roseland Gardens closed down for the evening.

People were drifting out to cars in lucky couples or sadly solo. Some were striking out walking on Flat Creek Road.

"Where're they all going?" I asked Atticus.

"Uphill is Montreat, the Presbyterian retreat. Downhill is the Baptist Ridgecrest, and the Blue Ridge Assembly, that's YMCA, is several miles to the southwest. There are also summer homes scattered through the valley: ancestral places where flatlanders have been escaping the heat since the early 1800s, and bringing their servants — whether slave or hired — with them."

"So they're just going to walk all that way?"

"Unless they have a car. The bus doesn't quite make it up here."

The young lady who was not yet Nina Simone was standing by the door, shaking hands and talking to people. Horace Rutherford was hovering near her in a protective fashion, shooing drunks along and accepting the congratulations of appreciative jazz-ophiles. Not-Nina took the white scarf from her head and flapped it like a towel. She was surely as sweat-soaked as any of the dancers. She turned and hung it on the doorknob behind her and returned to a conversation with a tall, balding man in a seersucker suit.

Dale Ray was three cars away from me, but we caught each other's eye: the scarf. It made perfect sense, numinescently speaking. We both started swimming upstream through the crowd like hungry salmon-sharks.

Dale Ray reached her first. "Excuse me, Miss. I just wanted to say what a great pleasure it was to hear you sing tonight."

He held out his hand. She looked at it as if appraising it's whiteness, raising one eyebrow in a sophisticated gesture of disdain, surprisingly sophisticated for one so young. She did not take the hand.

"It's okay, Miss Eunice," Horace said. "This is a friend, Mack the knife, I call him."

"Yeah? That's because he can cut in on *our* music, *our* place any time he wants to. But can I go see him play? Can I go to a white club? No I can not."

"You're right, Miss," Dale Ray said. "You are sure right about that. But don't you think we gotta believe it's gonna change some day?"

"When? You see all these men here? They fought in the war; they put themselves on the line to fight the Nazis. Then they come home to the same old… No, sir. If that don't bring change, I don't see nothin' that will."

"Miss Eunice played an audition for a school up North," Horace interjected. "Did a fine job, too. But they turned her down because of her skin color."

"Well, I believe that's wrong, lady."

"Humph. Did you know Mister Rutherford here shows movies for the children on Saturday morning, because the white movie house won't let them in?"

"Yes, I knew about that."

"I have never met a white man I could trust. There just aren't any."

As they chatted on in this amiable manner, I slipped behind them, miming to Horace that I'd left my hat. He nodded me in. I slipped the scarf off the doorknob as I passed. I went in to the hall and around and out through the kitchen. I put the scarf in my pocket. When I came back around to the front, Not-yet-Nina and Horace were gone. Dale Ray was holding up a drunk, to keep him from falling down. Atticus joined us.

"Anything?" he asked.

"What about this?" I said, showing him the scarf. "It's the singer's."

"Possible. Dale Ray, I don't think that man will fit in Odell's pocket."

"No, Atticus. This is Chick Dougherty. He partied a little too hearty tonight. Horace asked me if we could run him up to Miss Hall's place in Montreat. He has to be at work in a couple hours."

"Dale Ray."

"I said we would. You would, since you're the one with the car."

"All right, then. Let's go. We can drop him off, then get Odell down to Pellom's and see if his magic scarf will do the trick. Then I have to take Miss Wayman back into Asheville. She's waiting in the car."

Dale Ray and I shouldered Chick, who was humming happily, and we all trooped over to the Chrysler, which was now standing alone in the empty parking lot. Birds were singing in the trees and it was starting to get light in the east. Not-yet-Nina was sitting in the backseat, her head laid back on the seat. Dale Ray opened the door on the other side and I got in to pull Chick along.

"What's all this?" she sat up sharply. What's going on?"

"A little detour, Miss Wayman," Atticus said. "A mission of mercy. We need to take Mr. Dougherty here up the road a bit. As you can see, his ambulatory powers are a bit diminished."

"I am not about to ride off into the night in a car full of white men. I'd rather walk."

"Technically, you wouldn't be. Mr. Dougherty would be classified as, um, "colored." If you'll be more comfortable, you can ride up front with me."

"I'll sit right here. It's less likely the cracker sheriff will see me and pull us over for the wrong conclusions."

I ended up sitting next to her, with Chick, head lolling by the window. We thought that would be safer. There was ample room in the back of the Chrysler so that nobody had to touch anybody. Eunice turned away and stared pointedly out the window. We arranged Chick so his head was resting on the windowsill. I sat awkwardly in the middle. Dale Ray jumped in the front.

"And we're off!" he said, a little too cheerily.

Atticus got in and started the car, which purred like a giant mechanical circus beast. We drove up Flat Creek Road a half mile or so and turned right onto Montreat. There in the middle of the road was a stone gate with two arches. A wooden fence braced it on either side. The arches looked like a tight fit, built perhaps for less magnificent vehicles than the 1948 Chrysler Imperial.

As Atticus slowed to thread the gate, I felt funny. My hands and feet went numb and I was suddenly very dizzy. I looked at Not-yet-Nina and she seemed to be becoming transparent. She was looking back at me, wide-eyed.

"This man is smoking!" she said, alarmed, hugging the door even more.

Atticus turned to look over his shoulder. As he did so, the car scraped the side of the gate. He slammed on the brakes and we all lurched forward. Except I kept on going, through the front seat and through the dash. I looked at Dale Ray as I went by, feeling more confused than scared.

"Whoa!" Dale Ray shouted. "This is a gate!"

"What are you doing?" Eunice yelled, terrified. "I *knew* I couldn't trust white people!"

The car was fading away like fog. I put my numb feet down and they hit the road. I passed through the hood, grill and bumper of the car and turned in slow motion to reach back toward the others. I saw the faces of Dale Ray and Atticus, disappearing in the fog. Dale Ray looked worried, but Atticus was smiling. He mouthed the word "scarf" just before he disappeared.

I stumbled and fell onto the blacktop. I lay there for a minute, waiting for my head to clear. When I sat up, the Chrysler was gone. Long beams of sunlight were streaming overhead, exploding on the mountain to the west. The birds were singing like a mad whistler's choir. It was going to be a gorgeous summer day. I got to my knees just as a 1970's black and white police car rolled to a stop in front of me.

128 Jerald Pope

PART TWO: July 23, 1975

130 Jerald Pope

THE MONTREAT GATE, LATER

I heard the door open and footsteps coming toward me. I raised my head, feeling queasy. When I had time-traveled to Pellom's Time Shop, it had been instantaneous, and so painless as to go unnoticed. This time had been a weird, wrenching experience. I wondered what Atticus would tell Eunice/Nina—*told* Eunice/Nina, for that was now twenty-seven years in the past, if I was where it looked like I was.

"You all right?" A pair of boots under starched khaki pants asked. "Did somebody hit you?"

"Umph," I said, trying to get on my feet. The cop helped me up. I had a few scrapes and a bruise where my cheek had met the pavement, but was otherwise all right. "I'm not sure... I was walking along, and, all of a sudden, I was on the ground."

"Darn kids. They come speeding up through here, trying to thread the gate. What're you doing out so early?"

"Well, I was jogging…" I quickly stopped and searched my memory – was "jogging" a thing in 1975? Had it been invented yet? It was a word, I was sure. "…jogging along the road here. I have trouble sleeping, so sometimes I run, you know. I was a runner in college."

"College man, eh? I never saw the need. Do you think you'll be wanting a doctor?" He was smiling at me in a concerned way. He hadn't asked for ID or treated me with suspicion; this was very much a pre-9-11 kind of policeman.

"No, I think I'm okay."

"Did you get a look at the car? I'll bet it was that Graham boy. He lives up here in Montreat, and he runs plumb wild."

"I don't even know if it *was* a car. Maybe I just fell- tripped or something."

"Well, okay then. Where are you staying? I'll give you a ride; you probably shouldn't be running around here any more this morning."

Where was I staying? Clarice and her folks loved the Monte Vista Hotel. In 2013, we were staying there for the wedding. It was an old place; I hadn't seen it in 1948, but I was sure it was older than that, so it must be here in 1970-whenever. And I had a room key in my pocket. I took a chance. "The Monte Vista?"

"Yeah, I can drop you off there. You're lucky I was up here. I usually make a run up to the gate once or twice a day, then turn around back to town."

I got into the car, and we drove down the hill. I hadn't seen this part of Black Mountain before, but was reassured to see the Sixties and Seventies era cars parked in driveways and lining the streets. We passed a milk truck, the milkman carrying a rack of milk bottles from house to house, so some things were still foreignly antique.

I looked closely at the policeman for the first time. He looked familiar; a tall, raw-boned man with a satisfied set to his jaw. His uniform said he was the police chief, so Black Mountain was still small enough that the chief went on patrol. Then I realized who he was: the cop that had been cruising the young girl at the movie theater, Arthur Joe. I couldn't resist.

"I used to come up here when I was a kid," I said. "I remember a policeman back then, who this little high school girl was chasing. Aren't you him?"

He nodded with a tight grin, obviously used to being known in this context. "Yep. That's me."

"So what happened? Did she catch you?"

"Yeah, she chased me til I caught her. Mary. We've been married twenty-six years now. I was able to resist her til she went down with the appendicitis. I went to see her in the hospital, and she just looked so pitiful, lying there in that big old bed, her folks sitting around, worried to death. I just popped the question. She seemed to perk right up, too, after that."
"Congratulations."

"Well, she's a sweet little thing, and I do love her. Reminds me of a story. Man was working for the CCC, you know, during the

Depression. Civilian Conservation Corp? He was running a survey chain down in the Smokies. Now the CCC was run just like the army – they had uniforms, barracks, mess halls. And they gave all the men dopp kits, with combs and shaving gear and such in 'em. Had a little metal mirror in there too, for shaving.

"So this man and his crew were surveying way back in the mountains. One morning, he had set his mirror up in the crook of a tree and was shaving himself, when he sees an old mountaineer come walking up behind him. I mean this old boy was rough! Had long hair and a big old long beard, wearing a worn-out hat and overhauls. No shoes – I expect he never had a shoe on his foot in his life.

"Well, this old feller is looking at the shaving mirror with the curiousest expression on his face. The man turns around and greets him and the old mountaineer asks him what sort of thing that mirror was. It was plain he'd never seen one before, growing up so far back in the woods like he had. Well, the fellah just up and gives the mirror to the old man. It only cost about a nickel, and he could easily get another at the commissary. The old boy thanks him and goes on his way.

"A couple days later the man is out shaving, got his new mirror in the crook of the same tree, and here comes the old mountaineer. Only he looks like he's had the tar beat out of him! He's got two black eyes, a couple more teeth missing, a big knot on top of his head – and he's got that mirror in his hand.
The man says, 'hey,' and the old man says, 'I'm sorry, sonny, but I got to return this here thing to you.'

"'How come?' the man says. 'What happened to you?'

"'Well,' the old mountaineer says, 'I took that thing home to show my wife. She was in the kitchen, cookin' up some vittles, and I come in and say, 'lookit here, Minerva, if it isn't the spittin' image of my old pappy, what's been dead this many a year.'

"'Well she takes it, and looks in it, and then takes in to whalin' on me with the skillet. I tell ya, she turned me ever way but loose. And I'm yellin' what did I do? And she says, "that ain't your old pappy what's been dead this many a year. That's that red-headed hussy you been goin' around with!"'"

I squinted my eyes to take in the story. How did this story remind him of his own marriage? I wondered. Arthur Joe turned to me, very seriously, except for a twinkle he couldn't keep from his eye. "And that's a true story. Do you believe it?"

Now I was in a quandary. Did I say, yes, I believed this obvious tall tale, and look like a fool? Or did I say no, of course I don't, and risk offending an authority figure who would be very interested in my non-status in his time-space continuum?

"Sounds good to me," I said. He nodded, satisfied.

We pulled into the Monte Vista driveway and up to the front door. I got out and thanked him for the ride. And the story.
"Now, if you recall what kind of car it was hit you," he said, "like a '67 red and black Barracuda, you be sure and let me know."
"I will do that, Chief. I will do that," I said, and walked into the hotel where my room wouldn't be ready for another, oh, thirty-eight years.

136 Jerald Pope

THE MONTE VISTA

The lobby was laid out differently from how it had been – when? Yesterday? A worn, wine-colored carpet was collapsed on the floor; the lobby furniture was older, darker, and seedier. The only light came from the western windows and a shaded lamp on the front desk – which was new. Or old. A shady looking character was sitting behind the front desk, reading the paper. He had hair below his ears and a droopy moustache and was chewing a toothpick contemplatively. He had a badge that said "Hi, my name is," and then a piece of masking tape with the name "Don" written on it in magic marker.

"You're up early," Don said.

"Out for an early morning… stroll," I said. "Beautiful day."

I waved my key vaguely at him and started up the stairs. If I was lucky the key would still fit the door. And if I was even luckier, no one would be in the room. As I passed the clerk, I saw a headline near the bottom of the page – "Elvis Still Wows Them."

No! Had I missed him by one day? The blood rose to my face, particularly those parts of my face that were bruised.

I circled back to the desk, scanning the paper – Wednesday, June 23rd. "So, Don, you an Elvis fan?"

"Not particularly. I'm more into mountain music. I do like classic Elvis, though. Did you go to the concert?"

"No," I said, my heart sinking like a hunka burning love, "I missed it."

"Well, you still got two more nights."

My heart soared on little blue suede shoes. "Yeah, thanks. I hope to catch him."

I continued up the stairs to the first floor. The lock on our door was gone – or not there yet. The only place for a key was under the knob, where a skeleton-type key would fit. So much for bed. I wanted to connect with John Pellom, but he wouldn't be open for hours. I was also feeling pretty tired from the all-night event at Roseland Gardens. Sleep would be nice. Getting home would be nicer.

The halls in the Monte Vista are not like modern hotels, which feel more like slightly disreputable dystopian alleyways. Here chairs, tables, bookshelves created places to hang out when you weren't in your room. Pre-TV, the rooms were pretty much for sleeping. I dropped into a comfortable looking stuffed chair and was asleep in two seconds.

Three seconds later, I was awakened by something banging against my feet. I peeled my eyes open to the sight and sound of Don vacuuming the hall with an ancient Electrolux. He was deliberately knocking up against my feet with the wand.

"Lift," he said. I lifted my feet and he vacuumed under them.

"Down," he said. I put them down. "Locked out?"

"No," I coughed and cleared my throat to buy some time to clear my mind. "The, uh, wife's a snorer. You know how that goes. What time is it anyway?"

"Little past noon. I let you sleep as long as I could. I get in trouble if I don't do my chores. You know how that goes."

"Uh, yeah. Well, gee, I guess the wife is already out shopping. I better get going."

"Yeah, she probably is. Do you want breakfast? Or lunch? We've got a pretty nice all-you-can-eat. Fill up before you go 'shop-ping.'"

It was slowly sinking in my sleep-fogged brain that Don knew I wasn't a guest there. And he apparently thought I was a bum in need of charity. I thought about going back to the corner café; Sudsy and Dorcas were surely long gone, but I had a strong feeling the food would be the same. "Well, yeah, that'd be nice. I am a bit peckish. I can pay, you know."

"Oh, I know," he said, eyeing my bruised face, the hole in the knee of my jeans, and my lime green camo shoes. "Come on downstairs."

140 Jerald Pope

We went down to the immense dining room. Four or five couples and a few groups of businessmen were eating. A hot table ran the far end of the room, under a pretty good mural of mountains and laurels. The mural, I remembered, had survived until my time.

"If you wanna wash up," Don said, "there's a bathroom downstairs, back of the bar."

"Yeah, that'd be good," I said. "I could use a quick splash and a pee."

"Under the stairs, down through the beauty parlor, turn right in the bar, it's at the back."

I followed his directions. The beauty parlor was lit and apparently in use, but no beauticians were around. The bar was dark and silent. As I went by the end of the bar, I saw a woman sitting there, turning a whiskey glass around on the bar top. She had on what looked like a dark suit and a hat. I nodded, she nodded, and I made my way through the tables toward the restrooms I could dimly see in the back. It suddenly struck me as odd, her sitting there, drinking, in the closed, unlit bar. I turned around to look at her – but she was gone. Vanished.

I suppose she could have silently slipped away in the three seconds my back was turned, but all my senses said no. The hair on the back of my neck stood up like fresh spring grass. Suddenly, I didn't need to pee. I hurried back upstairs, looking for the woman along the way. Not in the beauty parlor, not on the stairs. I rushed back into the dining room and let out the breath I'd been holding.

I stood there catching my breath. Everything and everyone looked normal – eating, chatting. Was she another time traveler? Was the downstairs bar a gate, and I'd just seen her leap, or fade, or whatever it was they – we – do? Her clothes, in retrospect, were antique: forties looking, in fact. Was she following me through time? Some kind of inter-dimensional cop or something?

"You look like you've seen a ghost," Don said, holding two plates heaped with food.

Oh, of course. That explained it. A ghost.

We sat at a table by a window, looking out on the heating up summer day. The plate had ham, green bean casserole, potato casserole, cole slaw, and Waldorf salad – a typical southern health plate. A waitress came by and brought us sweet tea. The food was good.

"You know," Don said as we ate, "the pig is a very intelligent animal. I worked for the carnival for a while, ran a side show: Toby, the Sapient Pig. Did a mental act."

"Okay, I'll bite. How smart was he?"

"Oh, that was one smart pig. Toby could count to a hundred, do simple arithmetic – add and subtract – and he could read minds."

"How'd he do that?"

"Well, pig's throats aren't really set up for human speech, so we developed a code, made up of certain grunts and squeals and foot work. I had inherited Toby from an old man, Tolerable Lee

Lytle, used to live right here outside of Black Mountain. He had taught Toby's predecessor the basics, but Toby really took to communication. Him and me really connected."

"You said he could read minds…"

"Yes. That's when our act really took off. People had seen counting pigs, of course, and chickens, horses; but a *mind reading* pig, now that was something."

"I can imagine."

"I discovered his talent quite by accident. He always rode in the cab of the truck with me, at least when he was little. Oh, he loved to sit up there, his head out the window, wind in his bristles. He'd drool a lot, kinda like a dog; but I didn't mind, seeing the joy on his face."

"Sounds like you two really did hit it off."

"Oh, we did. So one night – it was foggy, I remember – I got separated from the rest of the carnival people. Lost, down around Saluda. Have you ever been back up in there?"

"No, I'm from Tennessee."

"Well, bless your heart. Anyway, I'm poking around in the fog, trying to find a sign or something, and I pull up on this little rise, out of the fog, and stop to look at my map."

I signaled the waitress for more tea. As she poured, Don went on with his story. She sat the pitcher down, and stood there, listening.

"All of a sudden, Toby starts making little grunting noises and scratching his hooves on the dashboard. Now we had long ago established that that was a no-no; no hooves on the dash, and I reminded him of that. But he wouldn't stop, and as I listened to him, it sounded like he was saying, 'Go! Go!' I mean, as best as a pig could – you had to really listen."

"But you were pretty familiar with Toby's language, so to speak."

"Not at that time. But it came to me what he was saying, and he was pretty het up, so I started the truck, and just as we pulled off that little rise, darned if a big old freight train doesn't come barreling through – right where we'd been parked. I'd stopped right on the tracks! But Toby *sensed* the train a'coming, and saved my very life."

"Well, that was fortunate, but maybe he just felt the vibration from the tracks. Animals are more sensitive than we are about those things."

"That's what I was thinking," the waitress said.

"That's what I was thinking, too," Don said. "But then, something else happened."

"I'll bet," I said.

"I was pretty shook up, as you can imagine. But I finally found my way into Hendersonville and stopped at a little roadside diner to calm my nerves with pie. Cindy, would you mind bringing me and my friend some of that good peach pie?"

"I will in a minute, Don. I'm interested in how this turns out."

"I understand," he said. "Well, I leave Toby in the truck – we had an understanding about that – and went in to this joint and ordered my pie. Now this is the exciting part. As I lifted the fork to my mouth to take the first bite, here comes Toby! He'd opened his door, got out of the truck, pushed open the diner door, rushed in, and he leaps up (he was smaller then, remember) and knocks the fork out of my hand!"

Cindy and I each raised an eyebrow at each other.

"I know, I know, it's hard to believe," Don said, "but somehow, Toby *sensed* that the pie was bad, and there was nothing for him to do but come busting in there and save my life."

"That *is* exciting," I admitted.

"But it doesn't stop there. Of course, the diner people were upset, this mere pig implying that their pie was unfit. But I noticed they threw the rest of it out. We got back in the truck, and I thanked Toby and told him how I appreciated him saving my life twice in one night, and then we took off for Waynesville, where the carnival was due to set up the next day.

"If you was to get us that pie, Cindy, I'll hold the rest of the story til you get back."

"You promise?" Cindy asked. "You said the peach, right?"

Don leaned over the table as she scurried off and said in a stage whisper, "She's very high-strung. I didn't want her to get too excited."

"I heard that, Don," Cindy called from the pie station. The acoustics were very good in that old dining room. She came back with three pieces of pie, handed them around and sat down. "Go on," she said.

"Well, I went on down to Brevard, then took out over the mountain to get to Waynesville. That's a pretty winding road, you know – pretty, but winding. You and the wife ought to check it out while you're down here."

"We'll do that," I said. "But get on with your story, Don."

"Oh, right. Well, we get to the top of the gap, and that old truck blows a tire. I pull over and set the hand brake. I get out and see the flat – it's the left rear. I'm pretty tired after all we've been through, but there's nothing to do but change out the tire. There's hardly any traffic up on that mountain, and for sure there's no gas station. So I get out the jack and the spare, jack up the truck and pull the tire. I get the spare on and am tightening the lugs when a big semi rumbles by. What he was doing up on that snaky road, I'll never know.

"Now, this is an old truck – mine, not the semi – and all I can figure is there was a mechanical malfunction. Apparently the vibrations from the semi cause the truck to lurch off the jack, and it starts rolling down the hill!

"Remember, I said I set the brake, and I did, but it's rolling anyway. It starts off slow, and I jump up, running along side, trying to get the door open. I see Toby sitting there, like a good pig – I told him to stay inside – but his eyes are as big as saucers, and he's looking at me like, 'what in the Sam Hill are we going to do now?'

"Well the truck is picking up speed, and there's a curve on a big old cliff coming up, and I'm barely hanging on to the door handle. As I try and get a foot up, my coat sleeve gets caught in the handle and all of a sudden, I'm being dragged along to my death! Out of pure desperation, I yell, 'Toby, for gosh sake, *do something!*'

"That was all he was waiting for. He slides over into the driver's seat, grabs the steering wheel with his teeth. I can't quite see, but he must have somehow worked the gearshift. He slams the truck into reverse and the whole thing skids to a stop.

"I get up and open the door and Toby just leaps into my arms (remember, he was a lot smaller then). Well, we hug and are just dancing around in the road out of the sheer joy of being alive.

"I get the lugs tightened on the wheel and we continue on down the mountain. I was a little put out with him for ruining the reverse on my transmission, but figured I would forgive him, his saving my life three times in one night and all. When we pulled into the campground in Waynesville, I turned off the truck and turned to Toby.

"'I just want to thank you, Toby,' I said, 'for what you've done tonight. It was exceptional.'

"He looked at me with those big blue eyes and said, 'Don, I know you'd have done the same for me.'"

There was a pause at the table while we all three sipped our tea.

"You mean…" Cindy started to say.

"Of course he didn't use just those words," Don said. "But I caught the gist of what he was saying. It was right then a true bond formed between us. We worked on our act and soon were the headliners of the carnival."

"Well," I said, "that's a marvelous story, and there's no doubt he was an exceptional pig. But I can't help but note that none of what he did could really be called mind reading."

"Oh that," Don said. "Well, that was just a trick, known to any good stage magician. I had certain coded signals I would give Toby. I'd say, 'Toby, this lady is holding an object in her closed hand. What could it be?' And depending on where I said 'Toby' or what phrase I used, like 'what could it be?' Toby would know it was a silver compact, or a pack of gum, whatever."

"So what happened to Toby?" Cindy asked.

"Oh, now this is the sad part of the story. As our fame spread, and we were earning more and more money, Toby took to eating; he was a pig, after all. And, well, he got fat. Too fat to travel. I mean he was upwards of five hundred pounds. I talked to him about it, but he said he had earned it, and he said, 'A pig, Don, must be a pig.' So I couldn't take him on the road any more. He couldn't even get in the cab of the truck – that was out of the question – and he loved that. It would have broken both our hearts to make him ride in the back with the chickens."

"Chickens?" I said.

"They were the opening act. So, as is traditional, I got a piglet and had Toby start training him to take over the act. But he was no Toby. I tried another and then another, but it was clear that there was going to be only one Toby. So we retired from the carnival business. I put Toby in a pretty nice barn and put the chickens to laying. I had to make some money to support both of us, especially with Toby's food habit.

"The egg business was going good, but I had to drive farther and farther every day to deliver the eggs. Then there came the fateful day – it was Mother's Day – that I decided to go down to Easley to see my mother. I had a neighbor, I thought I knew him pretty good, but I didn't know what he did for a living, and I asked him to take care of Toby while I was gone. That was the very words I used, 'take care of Toby.'

"Well, I come home from a very nice visit with Mom, and I go to say 'hi' to Toby, but he's not there. I look around the yard – no Toby. I look in the house – no Toby. Now I am starting to get a bad feeling. I go over to my neighbor's and ask him where's my pig.

"'I took care of him, like you said,' he said.

"'Well, where is he?' I asked.

"'Down to the store,' he says. 'Come on, I'll take you.'

"Well. To make a long story short, we ride down to his store, and as we pull up, I see what it is. A butcher shop. My neighbor was a butcher."

Cindy's mouth dropped open. "Don. No, don't tell me," she said.

"I was heartsick. I couldn't even go in there. He started to tell me what kind of cuts he'd made- roasts and pork chops and all; I just climbed out of his car and walked away. That was the day

I lost the best friend I ever had." Don took the last bite of ham from his plate, looked at it, sighed, and popped it in his mouth.

I was emotionally drained. I sure couldn't finish *my* ham. Cindy took a little lace handkerchief from her breast pocket and wiped her eyes.

"What's the damage?" I asked Cindy.

"I think my heart is broken," she said.
"No, I mean for the lunch."

"Oh, two dollars for you. Don's is free," she said. But she glared at him as if it shouldn't be.

I pulled three dollars out and laid them on the table. Don picked them up.

"Silver certificates," he said. "Haven't seen one of these for a while. Tell you what, I'll take one of these and put you on my tab. You can have the other two back; you might need them."

I shrugged and took the dollars back. I stood up. "Well, I better get going. See what that crazy wife of mine is up to."

Don looked at me with pity. I was obviously a delusional guy who had robbed grandma's button box to go on a quixotian search for a wife that didn't exist. That irritated me a little until I realized it wasn't far wrong. I bid them goodbye, then walked out into the brave new world of 1975.

150 Jerald Pope

PELLOM'S TIME SHOP

There were more service stations in town, selling forty cent gas to the sleeker, more variously colored cars of this new era. I passed the city hall and fire station. The city hall was still functioning, but the fire station was closed. I wondered if Dale Ray was still alive and still in jail. The funeral parlor was now a beauty parlor – a logical evolution.

The tourists were still very much in evidence. I suppose tourism was the one eternal truth of Black Mountain. Gone were the hats and gloves; come were the leisure suits and tailored bell-bottoms. A sartorial divide still separated children and adults; the leisure suit, for example, was an exclusively adult mistake. The occasional famous hot pants were to be seen, mostly – and fortunately – on teenagers and younger women. Grannies dressing like teenage hookers was a fashion quirk reserved for the twenty-first century. Shorts of all kinds – I didn't remember seeing any on the streets in 1948 – had "made the scene." Now men and women in Bermudas mingled with their more modish contemporaries.

As I turned on to Cherry Street, I noticed the American flags. They were everywhere – on cars, in windows, on poles outside businesses. The Fourth of July was long past. I reached back in my memory, what had happened in July, 1975? Were they celebrating Elvis' coming? What did I remember about *any* of 1975? The Centennial was next year… Then it came to me – Vietnam.

The war had ended that spring with the helicopters taking the people off the roof of the embassy in Saigon. America's first undeniable defeat, and by a little piss-ant country nobody had ever heard of! What other response could there be but flag-waving?

I found myself comparing things more to my brief sojourn in the Forties than to my true life in the Teens. People still smoked on the street, but it wasn't as universal as it had been in the Forties. There still weren't as many overweight people as in my era. The whole town and the people in it looked – "weary" is the word that came to mind – as compared to the energy and optimism gleaming from the faces of the Forties crowd. Stress was showing around the edges of the smiles, but clearly not as much as we had grown accustomed to in 2013. These folks had just endured Watergate and Vietnam; 9-11, the draining of people's savings every ten years by Wall Street, and the daily random shooting and/or bombing that were "normal life" in my time were still distant and unimaginable nightmares.

Other changes had come to Black Mountain. The Corner Café was now The Café on the Corner. They had added some hanging ferns, but otherwise it looked about the same. I thought I glimpsed a much older Dorcas behind the counter; the sullen Sudsy was nowhere in sight – I doubt he could have survived this long, given his spleen.

A Harley thumped by, the long-haired rider clad in dirty leather, with a similarly clad and similarly dirty-looking woman riding behind him. This was the outlaw biker that Marlon Brando and Peter Fonda celebrated. It would be decades before the sight of a squadron of heavy American iron coming down the road would raise the cry from the local populace, "Look out! Doctors and lawyers coming!"

An orange muscle car turned the corner, going down Cherry Street, the driver's T-shirt clad arm hanging out the window, a cigarette pinched casually and eloquently in three fingers. The GTO's engine throbbed to a different beat than the Harley's. Barry Manilow's "Mandy" played on what was surely an eight-track and blasted out an improbable counter-melody to the car's big engine.

Pellom's Time Shop looked the same – same sign on the window, same clocks inside it – only a little dustier, a little less organized than it had been a quarter of a century before. The shops around it had changed. A bookstore stood on one side, and "La Mode" dress shop on the other. A hand-lettered sign on the door said "Be Right Back." I had slept the morning away and was anxious that I might miss Elvis. I figured he, being a rock-and-roll god, was probably a late sleeper too, but I couldn't afford a mistake. This was my one chance to get back home.

"There you are," a voice said from behind me. I turned to see a short man in his late fifties, with thick glasses, and his hair combed straight back over his shining pate. He leaned past me to unlock the door. "I wondered if you had made it or not. Today's the day."

"John," I said. "Did I miss him?"

John led the way inside and pulled the string to turn on a big overhead fan. The store was definitely more chaotic than before. A pile of alarm clocks huddled on a table; I thought the grandfather clock standing open by the workbench was the same one that had been there in the late Forties. John was apparently an exacting, if not a swift, craftsman. "I don't think so. He played his first concert last night. Apparently went very well. He's staying at the Rodeway Inn over on Tunnel Road. I'm not sure why he'll be coming to Black Mountain instead of to town; maybe to avoid the fans or somesuch."

"How am I going to get in there? How am I going to get the tooth?"

"That's up to you," John said, appraising me over the top of his glasses. "Once you get it, bring it back here – that's all I know for sure. Did you learn anything from Atticus Crow, or – what was his name?"

"You mean Dale Ray?"

"Sure. That was it. He's been gone for probably twenty years now."

"What do you mean, 'gone'? Dead, or…?"

"Or. He just disappeared one day. Nobody's seen him since. Not that he was missed that much."

"And Atticus?"

"Retired from the lawyering business. Moved to Florida, I'm thinking."

"Okay. Well, I'd better get going."

"I don't think there's a hurry. I just had lunch with Doc Love. He didn't know anything about Elvis' coming. The office will be locked."

"Hm. Okay. Hopefully I'll see you in just a little bit. Stay open for me."

"Oh, I will. I've been waiting for this day for a long time."

156 Jerald Pope

DOCTOR LOVE

I walked down the street toward the bus station, which incongruously had motorcycles parked in front. As I got closer I saw the bus sign was gone; now a funky, hand-painted sign proclaimed the place to be "McDibbs." Handmade posters for various unknown bands were taped to the windows: "Razor's Edge," "Lefty's Dilemma," "Electric Toothbrush." The smell of beer and cigarettes oozed out the open door. As I passed, I peeked in and saw a couple of leather clad bikers shooting pool with overall clad locals. There was peace in the valley.

I walked on down to the train station. The newsstand and shoeshine boy were gone. The station was still open, but looked bedraggled, as if it hadn't had any serious attention in years. Many of the stores along Cherry Street were empty or had thrift store "antiques" for sale. As I stood on the corner, a train came in from the east; a diesel passenger train with only three cars. It stopped and sat there, its engines whining. No one got off, no one got on, no one came out from the station. After an eerie five minutes, it started up and left. The whole thing was like an episode from the Twilight Zone, or the Twilight Series; spooky and sad at the same time.

I turned down Sutton Avenue toward Broadway. I saw that the Interstate had been completed, tearing through what had been farmland south of town. Broadway now extended across the tracks and was on its way to becoming the main street into town. I walked up the hill, passing the blond brick building with Doctor Love's shingle hung in front. His office was upstairs above a flower shop. A closed sign hung in the door. I tried the knob; it was locked. I looked around to see if anyone was watching. A group of women wearing matching red T-shirts that said something positive about Jesus were coming down the hill toward me, each licking an identical ice cream cone. They seemed oblivious to my presence, let alone my potential larceny. Just in case, I held my hand to my jaw and moaned theatrically as they passed.

I went on up to State Street. Avena's was gone, as was the Pix. The furniture store on Broadway had begun its take-over of the eastern block, a Blob of Home Furnishings, devouring everything in its path. The soda fountain in the corner drug store was crowded. This was where the Christian ladies must have gotten their cones. The hardware store next door was open, looking not that much different than it had in the Forties. A life-sized cutout of a bell-bottomed Mod family selling paint stood in the window, but otherwise, it looked the same.

I tried the door that went upstairs to the dance hall, but it was locked and looked like it had been for years. Dirt, gum wrappers, bottle caps and old cigarette butts congregated around its sill, the detritus of a forlorn – if festive – social tidal wave.

I wandered into the hardware store. The wooden floor creaked as I walked the aisles. The place was properly packed with stuff, and dusty, as any good hardware store should be. Three old men, looking as creaky as the floor, stood around the register, their arms folded across their ample bellies, laughing. They stopped talking as I approached, eyeing each other with eloquent, silent looks that plainly said, "I got the last one. It's your turn." I stopped at a crowbar display and picked up a little crowbar called a catspaw. This I might need.

I took it to the counter and one of the geezers peeled off from his gaggle. "Find everything you need?" he asked.

"This is all I need."

"Then you, sir, are a lucky man." His cohort chortled dutifully at what was obviously a very old chestnut. He eyed the catspaw, turned it over a couple of times as if waiting for a psychic message. The message apparently came and he pronounced it's price. "Dollar fourteen, including the governor's share, for the fine job he's doing."

I pulled out my cash and was digging through the change when he said, "I'll take care of the hard part." He took four cents out of the take-a-penny-leave-a-penny dish. Another dutiful chuckle.

I gave him a dollar and a dime. When he saw the silver certificate, he slipped it into his pocket and pulled out a newer bill, which he deposited in an ancient wooden cash register occupying the place of honor on the counter. "You don't need a receipt," he stated.

Another old man in work boots, baggy jeans and a dirty yellow T-shirt that tried but failed to cover his tremendous belly came up from the back of the store. He was chewing tobacco and carried an empty soup can. "Gents," he said, and spit a long stringy loop of tobacco into the can. "Working hard?"

"Hardly workin', Ferrell," said one of the gallery. This elicited appreciative laughter all around. "You get that tractor runnin' yet?"

"Oh, yeah, she's a-runnin'. What're you loafers up to? No good?"

"Takin' her easy, Ferrell," said the other wingman.

"Yeah, I'll take it any way I can,' Ferrell quipped. This drew the most chuckles yet, along with murmured affirmations of "You got that right," and "I'm with you there, boy."

"Listen," Ferrell said, when the hilarity had subsided, "I got my honey-do list I'm working on. Thelma's gettin' ready to start cannin'."

"Mm. Tell her to save some of that apple butter for me," the lead comic said.

At this, Ferrell slid another rope of brown spit into his can – an unsettling juxtaposition with the idea of apple butter. "Naw," he said, "she's just doin' 'maters, okry, pickles, and string beans this year. She was laid up most of the winter, you know."

"I know. How's she doin'?"

"She's better. Old and wore out, like the rest of us."

"You got that right," the salesman said, shooting a quick resentful glance at me. I was the only person in the store under sixty and not 'wore out.' This was apparently my fault. "So," he continued, "what can we do you for?"

"Gimme three dozen quart cannin' jars, some lids and rings. And I guess I'll take a couple bags of layin' feed."

Suddenly the laconic trio was all action. One man went into another room and came back with the lids and rings. The second climbed a small but dangerous looking ladder and reached down all three boxes of jars at the same time. The remaining comedian – the one working the register – started ringing everything up. "You parked down back, Ferrell?" he asked.

"Yeah, I'll get the feed on my way out. You boys don't need to bother yourselves."

I remembered that the dance hall above had the rickety stairs leading to an alley in back; the alley where Dixie had held my hand. Doctor Love's practice must back up to the same alley. This might be my opportunity to get in and scope the place out before the king arrived. "I'm going out that way," I said. "I'll help you load it up."

They all paused, weighing the chance to avoid stairs and some heavy lifting against allowing a rank stranger to participate in the sacred hardware dance. Sloth won.

"I'd appreciate that, Mister," Ferrell said, paused significantly, then said, "You ain't from around here, are ya?"

"No, I'm kinda vacationing with the, um, wife and in-laws from over Knoxville way." I found my sentence structure sliding to fit in with the good ole boy vernacular. Why, I did not know.

"Well, that's good country," The cashier pronounced. And thus I was accepted. "Thanks for helpin' out."

I stuck the catspaw in my back pocket and went downstairs with Ferrell. We loaded the fifty-pound bags of feed in his truck, he spat in his can, we shook hands and he went on his way.

I sized up the back of the dentist's office. Not surprisingly, the rickety dance hall stairs were gone from the hardware building. A landing and stairs hung from its main floor, but they weren't near the office building. There was a narrow space, maybe four feet wide, between the doctor's building and the pharmacy, both of which fronted on Broadway. I saw a narrow window open above me. If I could wedge myself between the buildings, I could maybe walk up the wall and clamber in the window. There was a variety of pipes, electrical connections, and window sills I could use as steps along the way.

I started crabbing my way up between the buildings, bracing my feet, then pulling up with my hands until I could grab another hold with my feet. The span made it hard to do; I was effectively doing a sort of sideways pull-up. By the time I got to the window, my legs and arms were trembling, all to different rhythms. I pried the screen off the window with the catspaw and let it drop to the alley below. Grabbing the sill with both hands, I somersaulted into the building.

I was at the top of the stairs outside the office door. I wiped the sweat off my face onto my sleeve and the grime off my hands onto my pants. I tried the door- it was unlocked. Quickly and silently I slipped inside.

"Well, hi there!" a friendly woman's voice said. I spun around so fast I nearly fell over. "Easy there, cowboy. You having vertigo? Toothache'll do that, you know."

I smoothly recovered my equilibrium, stumbled over a chair, and coasted up to the receptionist desk. "Hi," I said. "You're open."

"Sure are," the receptionist, a small, well-packed bleached blonde in a white nurse uniform, said. "The Doc's not back from lunch yet, but he's due. Did you have an appointment?"

My mind was working fast. If I made an appointment, it would probably require my being in a dentist's chair with all that implied: drills, metal probes, pain. Drills. I wasn't prepared to weigh my getting back to my own time versus that, but knew it would take some serious consideration. Not a fan of dentist's chairs. Or drills. "Well," I said, to buy me some time. I heard the door at the bottom of the stairs open. The phone on her desk rang.

"Excuse me just a minute, honey," she said. She picked up the phone, listened for a moment, put the receiver to her chest, and screamed.

Footsteps rushed up the stairs. I turned around as Doctor Love, a medium sized man with dark hair, a sickly moustache, and horn-rimmed glasses rushed into the room, followed by an older woman with an enormous pile of red hair, harlequin glasses, and too much makeup. "What's going on here?" the doctor demanded. "Who are you?"

"Well," I said, to buy me some time. This was not going exactly like I'd planned it. And I hadn't planned it that well.

"Holy Moly, Doctor!" the receptionist shouted, jumping up from her desk and literally patting her hands together with excitement. "Elvis! Elvis is coming! Holy Moly!"

"Calm down, Candy," the doctor said. "We already know that. He was in Asheville last night."

"No, no, no! He's coming *here,* to the office. He needs a tooth pulled and they want us to do it!"

The red headed woman gasped like she'd just been sucker-punched and dropped into a chair, clutching her cheeks. Candy suddenly realized she was still holding the receiver to her chest. "Oh my gosh!" She took a deep breath, and said in a relatively calm and barely professional voice. "The doctor just returned. From lunch. I'm sure we can clear some time. Just let me check. Hold, please. Doctor, can you fit an extraction in. This afternoon. Right now. For *Elvis?*"

"Wow," the doctor said.

"Yes, sir," Candy said to the phone. "Whenever he can get here. He's on his way?" She turned her head from the phone and let out a squeal – tiny, compressed, but packing the full force of her fandom. "Well, that'll be just fine." She listened for a moment. "Of course. Of course. We understand. Completely professional. Thank you."

She hung up and squealed again. "Holy Moly! He's on his way! They're leaving the motel now! Oh, we can't tell *anybody*. He doesn't want any fans, any publicity. Just us. Oh my gosh, this is so exciting."

The doctor ran his fingers through his hair and checked himself out in a mirror behind Candy's desk. "Ruby, go clean the surgery. I want it spotless. Candy, clear the appointments for the rest of the day." At the mention of other patients, they all three realized I was standing there. They turned and looked at me. The doctor was brushing invisible crumbs off his tie in an unconscious attempt to make it look, somehow, more "showbiz." "You heard everything," he said.

"Well," I tried again.

"What did you need?"

"I can come back, when it's more convenient." Which is really *not* what I wanted to say. Or do.

"But you can't tell anybody. He doesn't want a crowd."

"Well."

"Maybe you better just stay here. As soon as I finish with… you know, I can get to you. After he's gone. Just have a seat. There's magazines, coffee, I really have to…"

"I know," I said. "I'll be fine." I sat down next to the redhead, who looked me hard in the eye, then stood up and rushed into the ominously named "surgery." The Seventies were apparently just on the cusp of the era of assembly line medicine. Doctor Love had only one chair, so I was spared the low-grade horror of sitting in the up-next torture chamber, speculating on the specific uses of the "instruments" displayed around the room. I never watched *Marathon Man*, knowing what it was about (dental torture, right?). My imagination created a movie that was sufficiently intolerable, thank you very much. As soon as I sat down, the frantic staff forgot me. This was better.

But I needed to get closer to the tooth. I couldn't imagine Elvis, or someone in his entourage, leaving that holy relic behind. By the mid-Seventies, the hagiography of Elvis was well under way. Sweaty scarves, uneaten sandwiches, all would be carefully preserved. An actual tooth from his actual mouth would be priceless. I imagined there would be body guards – at least one – or maybe a take-along lawyer, who would pocket the tooth for later disposal.

Candy was on the phone, cancelling appointments and swearing people to secrecy. Doctor Love rushed out of the back room, paused in front of Candy's desk as if about to say something, held up one finger, and rushed out. Ruby was bustling around, emptying trash, dusting, fanning her bosom with her hand, laying out tools – not necessarily in that order. I walked over to a magazine rack on the wall by the door to the back, pretending to look for reading material. I moved slowly and as unfocused as I could, trying not to make any move that would draw attention.

When Candy seemed the most distracted, I slipped into the back. The dentist's office occupied the whole top floor of the building. I was in a short hall with an office on one side, a break room on the other. At the end was the surgery. I could hear Ruby bustling around in there, humming "In the Ghetto." I stepped quietly into the office and partially closed the door, so I could see what was going on. When Ruby went out to the front office, I snuck into the surgery.

It was brightly lit, with windows facing the street. A small air-conditioner hummed in one of them. The chair, of course, held center stage, with two rolling stools in attendance. There were counters, a coat rack and two doors, one open and leading to a small bathroom, the other closed. I heard Ruby coming back. I wanted to hide in what I presumed was the closet, but there wasn't time. I was next to the bathroom, so I slipped in there. A toilet, a sink, and – surprisingly – a claw-foot bathtub crowded the tiny space. The dentist's suite had originally been an apartment.

The bathtub was neatly stacked with towels and napkins. Not exactly a sterile field, but – hey – this was dentistry pre-AIDS. Yet another future paranoia-inducing fact that we would just accept. I squeezed into the corner between the sink and the door. It was a lousy hiding place, but I was under pressure.

Ruby entered the surgery and walked directly into the bathroom, now humming "Viva Las Vegas." She certainly chose challenging songs to hum. She walked right past me to the tub and bent over to pick out the linen for the upcoming operation. As she stood and turned, she saw me. She jerked like she'd been shot and gave a little cry that was swallowed by a bigger gulp. She dropped the towels, sort of fell-sat on the edge of the tub, and clutched her breast. "What're... How... You're not supposed to be back here, you."

I started to help her, but realized lurching toward her at this moment might not be the best move. I stayed where I was. "I know," I said. "I just wanted to... Look, I'm a big fan. A huge fan. If I could just stay here, out of the way, and watch. I won't get in the way or anything."

"Absolutely not." She clambered to her feet, glaring at me. "You scared me to death." She reached up and rubbed her nose. It struck me like an electric shock...

Red-head, not blonde; old, not young; straight-toothed, not bucked (she was working for a dentist, after all): but absolutely her.

"Dixie," I said.

She froze, with her finger on her nose. "What? What did you call me? No, I know what you called me. How'd you know...? I don't go by that name any more. And who the hell are you?" Then she slowly lowered her finger.

I still had remnants of her lipstick on my mouth. I clearly remembered her smell, the texture of her hair, her eyes in the moonlight. Hidden under her blond bangs. It was like it was only yesterday. And for me, it was. For her, it was thirty years. "You wouldn't remember me. I just met you one day, at..." I nodded toward the back corner of the building, behind which stood the hardware store and dance hall above it.

"Well, that place is long gone. That life, too. I found Jesus, or He found me, and I was born again. There ain't no 'Dixie' any more."

"Okay, okay. I'm sorry I said anything. It just surprised me, is all."

"How do you even know about all that? I'm old enough to be your mother."

"Well, my mother used to…." I started a lie so outrageous, it died before I could get it out of my mouth. Besides, in that moment, I felt some loyalty to Dixie, to the woman who had been her and her kindness on that long-ago afternoon, yesterday.

"Look," I said. "Let's just start over. I don't want anything from you. Well, actually, I do. But from you, Ruby, not Dixie. I need… want to stay here and watch the, you know, operation."

"Elvis? No. Absolutely not. Now get back out front where the doctor told you to stay. And don't you dare mention…what you mentioned."

"I can't, Ruby. I mean, I'm such a big fan. Of Elvis, I mean. You know I follow him around, to see his show. I saw him in Knoxville, Atlanta, Charlotte. I'm probably his biggest fan." I was riffing as fast as I could, saying anything that came to my head. "He's not going to be with us that much longer, you know. He's going to be called home, soon. I know it, and every moment with him is just so precious – you know that too, I can tell. You're a fan…"

"I mean, I like him and all," she said. "You think he's gonna die soon? Really?"

"You know there are people that actually want him dead. People close to him. He knows things. Why do you think President Nixon called him to the White House?"

"Gosh, I remember that. I did think it was strange…"

I was rapidly getting to the end of what I knew about Elvis. I mean, I did like his music; he was the King, after all. But he was before my time. Our little tumble down the conspiracy rabbit hole was mercifully interrupted by voices in the reception room.

"Oh my god, he's here!" Ruby said. "Okay, it's too late now. You're gonna have to stay in here and stay quiet. If you make a peep, I'll scream and swear I don't know nothin'. You'll probably get arrested or something." She pulled the door closed, then cracked it open a bit and bustled out to meet the King.

I only had a moment and I needed to get closer. My completely-un-thought-through-plan had devolved into a snatch-and-run. As soon as the tooth hit the tray, I'd jump out, grab it, and run for Pellom's. Even if Elvis's men were hot on my tail, I only needed a second in the Time Shop, then I'd be gone.

The thought of what would happen if I *wasn't* gone tried to sneak into my brain, but I slammed that door fast. This had to work. I had to get back. This was my only chance.

I slipped across the surgery to the closet. I could hear Elvis's distinctive Mississippi baritone. "You boys wait out here. I'll be in good hands with the Doc and this purty little lady."

I opened the closet door, and nearly had a heart attack. The closet was occupied. I was staring face to face with Dale Ray. "What the h…" I managed to say, before he shoved me back into the room and closed the door.

I stumbled and fell to the floor. I scrambled to my hands and knees and tried to get back to the bathroom, but I could see the dentist's legs walking into the room. He was walking backwards and talking. I looked around in desperation. In the corner was one of those bentwood coatracks that were so popular in the Seventies. It was draped with several white coats and various random sweaters and jackets. A yellow umbrella was stuck in the ring at the bottom. It was a hopeless hiding place; but it was my last hope.

I slithered across the floor and behind the coatrack. Elvis was in the room – I could see the light glinting off his coal black hair. I put my back against the wall and pushed myself to a standing position. He was taller than I imagined, six feet or so. I had to crouch down about six inches to stay hidden behind the coats. He was wearing a dark blue jump suit with a white scarf tied around his neck. If anyone bothered to look, I was easy to spot, partially hidden behind the coats.

Doctor Love walked to the coatrack, reached out and took one of the white lab coats from it. His hand was three inches from my face. He wasn't looking – he'd made this move a thousand times- and there was a distraction in the room. I held my breath and tried to make myself smaller. My shoulders stuck out on either side, as did my bowed knees. My shoes shouted lime green and orange from the floor.

"No, I don't need no X-ray, Doc," Elvis said. "I know which little booger it is, no doubt about it. You just pull it, and I'll get a new one set in when I get back to Memphis."

Ruby was setting up the tray, breathless, her eyes locked on the Man in the Chair. All eyes in the room were locked on this god that had strode amongst them. I realized I could probably walk right by them and not be noticed. I relaxed a little and straightened my knees. I remembered Dale Ray in the closet.

What was he doing here? Well, that was obvious. He was after the tooth. Apparently he'd changed his mind about the pleasures of Forties living. But why would he want to go to *my* time? Unless the portal took different people to different times. I'd have to ponder this later. I wondered how many other people were hidden around the room – and where they could possibly hide.

"Normally, I'd have Doctor Nick just give me a little somethin' to get me by, ya know," Elvis was saying. "He travels with me, takes care of the band, anybody has any little aches or pains. It's a hard life, on the road; people don't realize. But we were foolin' around in the hotel after the show. I was showin' the boys this new little custom engraved Beretta I had. A pretty little thing; nickel and blue, ivory handles with my name on one side, Graceland on the other. Some Eye-talian dude gave it to me.

"So we had the TV on and there's this sci-fi movie – that's 'science fiction,' stories about space and time travel and all. And it's pretty sexy, French, has this cute space chick runnin' around havin' sex with robots and such, and all of a sudden I realize the space chick is *Jane Fonda*!

"Now, she is a real pretty girl and all, we even went out a couple times in Hollywood, but that chick is a traitor to America. I don't have to tell you. So I didn't even think about it- I just up and shot the durned TV! Only the bullet – it was only a little thirty-two – ricochets around and hits Doctor Nick right in the stomach!

"Well, I blame Jane Fonda for that. I would never have shot the TV if Hanoi Jane hadn't showed her Commie face on it."

"Did, um, Doctor Nick live?" asked the self-interested Doctor Jim.

"Aw, after the bullet bounced around inside that TV set for a while, by the time it hit Doctor Nick, it could barely pierce the skin. He was sort a surprised, no doubt about it. He fell down, we all got quiet for a minute – just kinda watching the blood drip. But then he looks up, says, 'not to worry. I'm a doctor.' Well, we all got a good laugh outa that – these boys are all a fun bunch to be around. He goes in the bathroom, operates on himself or somethin', I don't know, comes on back out after a while and picks up his drink like nothin' ever happened."

"So," said the not-too-relieved Doctor Love, "do you want gas, Mister Presley?"

"Bring on the nitrous! I love that stuff!" said the King, settling back in the chair, as Ruby pinned a napkin on his chest and unconsciously petted his arm. "But seriously, my kung fu training has brought to me a high tolerance for pain. It takes a lot of serious medicine before I even don't feel anything."

It is a stark lesson in the abject power of stardom that both Doctor Love and Ruby nodded their heads sagely at this nonsense. They strapped the mask on and Elvis kept making "higher" signs with his hands until he achieved the level of kung fu pain toleration that he was seeking. The light went on, the chair went back, and the most famous lips in the world were propped open as the dentist went to work.

Doctor Love was humming "Suspicious Minds" as he worked. Apparently humming was inherent to dental work. Ruby joined in as she passed him tools, sponges, and rinsed the King's mouth. After a moment, Elvis himself joined in the humming. That was a moment you won't hear on any bootleg recordings!

The tooth would be out in a moment. I needed to get ready to grab it, deal with Dale Ray, and whoever else might be lurking around, get through the body guards in the waiting room, and hot foot it around the block to Pellom's. I was already exhausted; I wasn't cut out to be an action hero, even a slow action one.

"Here we go," the doctor said. He braced himself on the arm of the chair and gave a mighty heave. Nothing. "Obviously, I want to get it all in one piece." Obviously, the doctor had his plans for the tooth as much as the rest of us. Damn. He climbed up onto the arm of the chair and leaned over the King, who was still humming happily.

Doctor Love grabbed his pliers with both hands and yanked and twisted. With a sickening grinding, sucking sound, the tooth came free. He held it up in the light, like Arthur presenting Excaliber to the world. The light gleamed off the gold cap.

Suddenly the window right beside me shattered into the room. Everyone turned toward it in shock, including me. A guy I'd never seen before started to clamber through the broken glass, his left hand wrapped in a Holiday Inn towel. There was a beat, then Dale Ray came rushing out of his closet toward the doctor, who fell back off the chair where he'd been perching.

The window guy was having trouble getting through the broken window – he cut his knee badly and started bleeding. It was time for me to join the fray. I stepped out and gave the window guy an elbow in the face. He yelled and fell back outside.

The door opened and a large man in brown aviator sunglasses and an Elvis-like pompadour burst in, yelling, "Boss! Boss!" He was followed by a much smaller man in a flattop and sideburns, holding a gun. Ruby was screaming and backing toward the wall.

Elvis raised his head, the gas mask over his nose, tubes and cotton hanging from his mouth, and said something like "coowah."

Somehow, Doctor Love still had the pliers, which somehow still gripped the tooth. Dale Ray had him by the forearm, reaching for the pliers, which the doctor held above his head, just out of Dale Ray's reach. Aviator-glasses grabbed Dale Ray by the shoulders and flung him across the room and against the wall. It was an amazing feat – sending such a big man literally flying. Dale Ray immediately leapt up and head-butted Aviator-glasses and they both tumbled to the floor, on top of the doctor.

Flattop scanned the room. Window-man was climbing back in, Ruby was still screaming, I raised my hands and shrugged like

I had no idea what these crazy people were up to. Elvis was half-sitting, pulling tubes from his mouth, but holding the gas mask firmly in place.

Flattop aimed his gun (was that a nickel-plated 32 automatic?) and fired at the window man. The noise from the gun made everybody freeze for a second. "Are you kidding? You're *shooting* at me?!" window-man said, and ducked below the sill.

Flattop shoved past the wrestlers and screaming Ruby to our side of the room. "Who are you?" he said, sticking the gun under my nose. These boys were sure serious about their body guarding.

"I'm the state dental inspector. Just doing my job," I improvised. "Who are you?" Lame, but it seemed to work. He turned and started beating the fingers of the window man who was hanging on the sill.

Doctor Love crawled out from beneath the wrestling men (Dale Ray now seemed to have the upper hand, and was pummeling Aviator-glasses in the head) and pulled himself up the side of the chair. His professional concern for his patient was impressive, given the three-stooges goings-on in his surgery.

He had dropped the pliers and I saw the tooth peeking out from under a sideboard.

I tried my invisible ninja move, sidling around the doctor toward the tooth. It didn't work. "What the heck are *you* doing in here?" he said to me, as he engaged in a tug-of-war with Elvis over the nitrous mask.

"It sounded like you needed help," I said, still sidling. "I heard all the commotion and came running."

"The hell he did," said Dale Ray from the floor, now strangling Aviator-glasses. "He's after the tooth. I came to stop him."

At that we all three scanned the floor for the tooth. My knowing where it was gave me a split second advantage. I scooped it up and jumped over Dale Ray, headed for the door.

"No you don't," said Dale Ray, and grabbed my pant leg. I popped the tooth in my mouth, which was – yes, I know – disgusting. But I needed my hands free. I grabbed the doorframe and pulled. Aviator-glasses wrapped his arms around Dale Ray and Doctor Love made a dive across them for me. For a moment, I was the lead contestant in a human tractor pull, dragging three grown men behind me down the hall.

Window-man made a grab for Flattop's gun. Another shot froze the assembled multitude again. In the lull, we could hear Elvis singing, "caught in a trap, we can't back out" and giggling in the chair. Even under gas, you could tell the man had an awesome singing voice. No wonder he was the King.

Ruby suddenly seemed to tire of screaming. She grabbed the stainless steel instrument tray, dumping the instruments on the floor. "Stop shooting that gun, you idiot!" she shouted. "You're going to hurt somebody!" Which seemed the point in shooting a gun, but I appreciated her concern. She then slammed Flattop over the head with the tray.

"Ow!" he said, turning to her and holding his head. "Lady, that hurt!"

"Well it was *supposed* to hurt," she said, raising the tray for another attack.

"You deserve it for beating my fingers with your stupid gun," Window-man joined the discussion.

It seemed like the party was winding down, so I thought it best to get going. I spat the tooth into my hand, jammed it in my pocket, stomped on Dale Ray's hand and twisted free.

"Otis! Take me with you!" Dale Ray shouted from the floor as I sprinted down the hall and into the receptionist's office.

Candy was on the phone and looked up guiltily as I ran past. "I'm not doing anything," she said.

"I don't blame you," I said and took the stairs four at a time.

PELLOM'S TIME SHOP

I was feeling optimistic as I hit the street. I had the tooth; all I had to do now was get to Pellom's and hope the magic worked.

I could hear feet pounding down the stairs. I didn't know whether it was faster to go up to State Street, then down Cherry, or down to the alley and up that way. In 2013, the alley had cut all the way through the block, but I couldn't remember if it did in 1975. It seems like there had been a building blocking the way in 1948. No time to back track if I chose wrong; I ran up toward State.

It was still a hot, sunny day with a goodly amount of people out and about. As I turned the corner at the pharmacy, I slowed to a brisk walk, hoping not to draw too much attention. I turned on the corner at Cherry, looking back at the commotion moving through the crowd toward me. I couldn't tell if it was two or three men pursuing me. Just as I started to sprint the last hundred feet to Pellom's, I bumped into Arthur Joe coming out of The Café on the Corner, eating a piece of apple pie. I knocked the pie out of his hand and we both watched it splat onto the sidewalk.

"Whoa! Slow down there, fellah," Arthur Joe said. "Oh, it's you. What's your hurry?"

"Thank god I found you!" I said, grabbing the tall policeman and pushing him toward State Street. "These guys are chasing me. They have guns!"

To his credit, Arthur Joe – who wasn't carrying a gun – put on his John Wayne face and immediately turned toward my pursuers. His intervention would buy me all the time I needed. I broke away and walked quickly down Cherry.

As I approached Pellom's, I saw Dale Ray coming up Cherry Street toward me. Dang. The posse had split up. Arthur Joe had Elvis' boys, but I still had to deal with my old pal, Dale Ray.

"Just hold on a minute, Bodell," Dale Ray came toward me with his hands raised. "I just wanna talk."

"Like heck you do," I said, continuing toward him. "You want the tooth."

"No, no. I just… I got in some trouble back in fifty-two. Moonshine, Federales. They weren't going to leave me alone. Just gimme a minute…"

He was reaching toward me, as if to take my hands. I knew if he got a hold, I'd be in for another tussle. I didn't have time for that. Plus, having seen how Dale Ray beat down the big bodyguard, I was pretty sure I'd come out on the losing end of that fight. I took a step back, then remembered the catspaw in my pocket. I took it out and as he got close, brought it down hard on his forehead.

He stopped and looked at me, disappointment in his eyes. "Aw, Otto. I thought we were…" Then he collapsed like a dropped bag of wet compost.

I felt a moment of pity for Dale Ray. He had helped me to get this far. But I wasn't giving up my seat on the future express for him. In retrospect, 1975 was better for him than 1952. He was a resourceful guy. He'd make it. The moment of pity was over.

"Nice one," said John Pellom, who was leaning in the door of his shop, watching us.

"I didn't want to do that," I said.

"Your kind never does." He smiled enigmatically, his eyes looming large in his thick glasses.

"What is that supposed to mean?" I said pushing past him into the Time Shop. "No, never mind. I don't care what it means. I just want to go." We paused. "Why aren't I going? I've got the tooth. It's the key, isn't it?"

"Yes, but maybe there's more to this one than just a key."

"What? What?" I could see Dale Ray stirring on the sidewalk. People were looking and pointing up the street toward where I'd left Arthur Joe and the bodyguards.

"You know. 'You've always had the power to go back to Kansas.'"

"No I haven't! Come on, John!"

"Well, you're right, you probably haven't. I just thought it would be funny to say that. There must be an incantation, some words that make it work."

"You mean like Abracadabra or something?"

"Well, I guess it's not Abracadabra. Try something else."

"Oh, come on, John. It could be anything. I'm never going to guess some mumbo-jumbo gibberish."

"Suit yourself. Looks like your friends are almost here."

He was right. The commotion in the street was moving closer. Dale Ray was sitting up, holding his head.

"All right," I said. "Uh, presto-chango. Mumbo-jumbo. Hokie-pokie. Higgledy-piggledy. Please-and-thank-you. I'm not good at this! Help me!"

"You really aren't, are you? Maybe something more connected with the tooth." John reached over and locked the door.

Dale Ray was on his feet, looking at me. He seemed unhappy. Arthur Joe was rattling the doorknob, the two bodyguards behind him, none of them looking too pleased.

"You mean dental phrases? Filling! Cavity! Drill! I don't know. It's not working, John!"

Arthur Joe was rapping sharply on the glass, beckoning toward John. Dale Ray seemed about ready to break the window.

"Hmm," John said. "How about some phrases connected with Elvis? That might work."

I gritted my teeth. "Oh, god. I want to go home! Hound dog! Blue suede shoes! Viva Las Vegas! Elvis has left the building! Uh huh huh!"

All four men were now yelling and pounding on the door. John looked at me apologetically and said, "I think I better let them in before they break the door."

"Bippty boppity boo! Partial plate! Jailhouse rock! Klaatu barada nikto! I'm all shook up! There's no place like home! There's no place like home! Oh, sweet Jesus, there's no place like home!"

A fog began to fill the room. Whether it was any of those words, all of them, or something else altogether, I'll never know. John opened the door and the crowd rushed in. Arthur Joe got a solid hold on my arm, but then his eyes widened in astonishment as his hands sank through me. The bodyguards jumped back as if they'd seen a ghost. Dale Ray had tears in his eyes as I faded away.

184 Jerald Pope

PART THREE: August 21, 2013

186 Jerald Pope

PELLOM'S TIME SHOP

"Are you enjoying your vacation?'" the old man behind the counter said. This was the John Pellom I remembered; nineties, thin streaks of hair combed straight back, short and stocky, but still with that sly, knowing twinkle in his eye.

"It has its moments," I said, brushing the dust off my pants. "Say, do you remember a guy named Dale Ray Something, used to hang around, kind of a ne'er-do-well?"

"Dale Ray Lee?" John's twinkle shifted into high gear. "I seem to recall he was mayor of Black Mountain for two terms back in the Eighties. Went up for bid-fixing: throwing his buddies fat contracts. Golf course, trash pickup, stuff like that. Good old boy network, you know."

"Not surprised," I said.

"You need anything? Watch battery? Watch band? Cuckoo clock?"

"No, I think I'm good. Thanks for everything, John."

I stepped out onto the street – the 2013 street – and breathed the slightly polluted, slightly desperate air of my time. It tasted like home. People were moving with purpose, shopping hard. Children and teens were plugged into their electronic umbilicals, ignoring their plainly clueless ancestors. Uncomfortable electric cars and overflowing recycling bins exuded their forlorn hope that there would be a future. I felt the old, familiar tension flowing into my shoulders. For all its threadbare heartiness, this was where I belonged.

The Elvis Tooth 189

190 Jerald Pope

TOWN HARDWARE

I pulled out my phone to check the time: 4:35. I couldn't remember what time it was when I went into the Time Shop that first time. Seemed like it hadn't been long. As I was looking at it, the phone rang.

"Odell, do you know what time it is?" my fiancée asked. I had to laugh.

"Hello, sweetie," I said. "Why yes, it's 4:35. And a half. Where are you?"

"We're at the hardware store. I miss you! Where did you get off to, baby?"

"Oh, I've just been sort of taking a ramble down history lane. It's an interesting town."

"Well, where are you now?"

"Cherry Street. I spent a little time in Pellom's Time Shop."

"Yelch. That place. You know one of Mother's friends told us about a lady who took her cuckoo clock in there to be fixed. She's been dead for three years now and it's still not ready."

"Yeah, it is kind of a clock graveyard in there. Time has no meaning at the Time Shop."

"Well, Daddy's getting hungry. Come meet us here, and we'll go eat."

"Okay."

"We're buying some gifts for Kenny's kids. You know, the kid's table. They have all these old-timey toys – really brings back the good old days."

"Mm. Okay, I'm on my way." I hung up and strolled up the hill. The shops had changed over the years, but still performed their ancient function of giving the people what they thought they needed. I passed the little independent bookstore, sandbagging the flood of digitalized illiteracy with slabs of paper. The okay pizza place, where we'd probably eat again, sent its siren smells wafting across the street. The Corner Café/Café on the Corner was now a mountain-trendy gift shop. A big semi rumbled by on State Street, like a whale going up a salmon stream.

I passed the stuffed cat store and paused a moment by the door to Dixie's upstairs nightclub. The cement was crumbling from between the bricks, the swirl of trash had grown in front of it.

This secret heart of Black Mountain was long forgotten. I wondered what its new secret heart was.

A little bell – a leftover from the Forties – rang as I opened the door to the hardware store. The store was transformed. Toys, camping gear, and souvenirs – the sort of trivial diversions you'd only buy on vacation – crowded the front. The real hardware was compressed by the tourist stuff into the back half of the store. As I looked for Clarice, I saw the hardware empire had expanded to take over the drugstore and the five and dime, the stores on either side.

I went into the former pharmacy, now full of postcards and kitchen stuff. I found Clarice and her folks standing, rapt, in front of a rack of fierce-looking cooking devices.

"I haven't seen one of these in years!" Ursula, the mother-in-law, barked happily.

"I remember my old granny used to use one all the time," said Van, the father-in-law.

I had no idea what it was or what it could be used for.

"I'm going to get it," said Ursula. "It'll make a funny gift for Anne. Getting my Christmas started!"

"Hey, stranger," Clarice said, grabbing me and giving me one of her special we're-the-only-people-in-the-world kisses. "Seems like you've been gone forever!"

"More like sixty years." I said, kissing her back hungrily. "I really missed you!"

"Gosh! What happened to your face?" Clarice touched the bruise on my cheek where I'd skidded into the Seventies.

"Ow," I flinched from her touch. "I wasn't paying attention where I was going. I turned around and ran into something. A light pole thing."

"Well, that's going to look great in the wedding pictures," she pouted.

"I'm sorry, honey. Maybe it'll fade by the wedding."

"Mm. It does sort of look sexy. Like you're a big rough and tumble dangerous adventurer."

"This I like," I said, petting her perfect, un-blemished cheek.

"Get a room, you two," Van said.

"Van!" said Ursula, slapping his arm, "they're not married yet!"

"Actually, we *have* a room," I said, giving Clarice one of my special we're-the-only-people-in-the-world bottom squeezes. She looked in my eyes, and I really was home.

"I'm not feeling that hungry," she said. "For food. Why don't you guys go on to the restaurant and we'll catch up with you later."

"Oh, for god's sake!" Van sputtered. But he was smiling.

"Remember, it's bad luck to see the bride naked before the wedding," Ursula said, kissing her daughter on the cheek, and tearing up. "My little girl!"

"Has turned into a horndog," whispered Clarice as we walked away. "Just let me get these cards to put in the memory book, and then…"

"Okay, but hurry up. Don't buy stamps."

We went up to the counter where an old-timey register frame hid a new-timey computer. A short woman in glasses and long brown hair was behind the register, sticking price tags onto Star Trek lunch boxes. I hadn't known they had to bring their lunches on the Enterprise.

"You've got a great store," Clarice purred, her hand in my hip pocket. "We love it."

"Thanks, sweetie," the woman said. "Where are you'ns from?"

"Knoxville," I said.

"And you're nearly newly weds."

"How'd you know that?!" Clarice laughed.

"Oh, I know lots of things," the woman said, and wiggled her eyebrows at me.

We laughed.

"Okay, that'll be six dollars and fifty-four cents."

Clarice pulled some bills out of her purse, then turned to me. "Do you have any change, Odell?"

I reached into my right pocket and pulled out an old popsicle stick, Nina Simone's sweaty scarf, and a bloody, gold-capped tooth with a hole in it.

"Oo, yelch! Odell! Where'd you pick up that old stuff?" Clarice wrinkled her cute nose in disgust.

"Around?" I said, not very convincingly.

"Well, why in the world....?"

"You want me to throw that away for you?" The woman held out her hand. I saw her right eyebrow go up a millimeter – maybe two.

"No, I think I'll hang on to it," I said, raising my own eyebrow and stuffing it all back in my pocket.

"Odell, you are so weird," Clarice said.

"You'd be surprised," I said, hugging her.

"I hope so," she said, kissing my left shoulder. Did I mention she was fairly short? And massively cute?

I reached into my left pocket and pulled out a wad of change and bills. I had three dollars in silver certificates, two silver quarters, a silver dime and a solid copper penny. "You know, we're in a hurry. Let's just put it on the credit card. You take American Express?"

"Surely do," the woman said. I thought I saw a little smile cross her face. Clarice ran her card. As the woman bagged her purchases, she said, "You young people are always in such a hurry, if you don't mind my saying so."

"Well, gosh," Clarice said, taking the bag and my hand, "it's not like we have all the time in the world! Do we, honey?"

"We'll see," I said, kissing the top of her head. "Maybe we do."

THE END

198 Jerald Pope

Acknowledgements

Thanks to:
David Billstrom
Cecil Bothwell
Susan Brackett
Katherine Debrow
E.V. Gouge
Mary & Arthur Joe Hemphill
Sheridan Hill
John Pellom
Tim Perry
Madeleine Pope
Don Talley
The Swannanoa Valley Museum
Rebecca Williams

Special Thanks to the Most Careful of Editors:
Teresa Luckman

Disclaimers, and What is Real

This is a work of fiction. It is made up. While I use some names and places from Black Mountain for verisimilitude, as far as I know they are not like the places and characters in this book at all.

REAL:

Pellom's Time Shop (opened in 1948).
German prisoners of war were kept in camps all over Western North Carolina.
There was a sort of a "performance venue" above the hardware store.
I've heard the portable jail cell story from more than one person.
The drive-by viewing window at the funeral home.
Avena's Bowling Alley
The Pix
The story of Mary's pursuit of Arthur Joe was told to me by Mary & Arthur Joe.
Merce Cunningham didn't come to Black Mountain College until 1953.
The hitchhiking cousin story is from E.V. Gouge.
Roseland Gardens
Elvis did have a tooth pulled in Black Mountain.
By Dr. Love.
Elvis did shoot out a TV at the Rodeway Inn.
The ricochet did hit his personal drug provider, Dr. Nick.

NOT REAL (as far as I know):

Time travel

200 Jerald Pope

Made in the USA
Columbia, SC
31 May 2017